MADE IN L.A.

MADE IN L.A.

Vol. 5: Vantage Points

MADE IN L.A.
Vol. 5: Vantage Points

Fifth Annual Anthology

Cover design by Allison Rose

Visit Made in L.A. Writers online at
www.madeinlawriters.com

ISBN: 978-1-953954-04-6

Published by Resonant Earth Publishing
on behalf of
Made in L.A. Writers
P.O. Box 50785
Los Angeles, CA 90050

CONTENTS

INTRODUCTION

In Los Angeles, the only constant is change. Our lives go through cycles and rotations. We incorporate new ideas, people, workplaces, and patterns into our lives: creating, destroying, amending, growing, persisting. To solve the problems and dilemmas in our modern lives, we have to look at them from new angles. The stories within this anthology show how Angelenos take actions, make choices, and reinvent themselves by imagining their options — and the ensuing consequences — from different vantage points.

You've read about our unhoused neighbors in our previous anthologies. In this volume, a different perspective emerges in "The Couch" by Christina Hoag, which follows an LAPD officer struggling to find herself shelter after she leaves a crumbling relationship. A parallel yet distinct tragedy is told in "Ghost of Central Avenue" by Jovon C. Johnson. This story immerses the reader in pain, a love story that haunts and lingers.

The vantage points in other stories provide glimpses from the perspective of train riders and pedestrians. "Riding the Blue Line" by Mary Anne Perez shows us a day in the life of a long commute and the unfolding of many stories carried within train cars. "Trouble Helping" by J.P. Higgins imagines a life-changing act of kindness that many have dreamed of with an outcome no one expects. "Window Walking" by Ryane Nicole Granados provides tantalizing glimpses of domestic scenes from the vantage point of two young girls on a sidewalk stroll.

We are also drawn into the past in this anthology. "Hollywood Endings" by Frank Castelluccio is a tragic examination of a gay couple's relationship deteriorating under the strain of mismatched expectations. "Epic Stick" by Thea Pueschel takes us inside a character's nostalgic ride that ends in misery. "Come as You Are" by Ryan Shoemaker is an ambitious, hard-rocking imagining of the final days in the life of Kurt Cobain and his encounters in Hollywood and the San Fernando Valley.

In several stories, evolving relationships take center stage. "Half-Buried Hearts" by Hazel Kight Witham looks at how a teenager's friendship crosses racial divides even as her father remains stuck in his prejudices. "Looking for Joey" by Tisha Marie-Reichle Aguilera follows a sister's desperate search for a missing brother after their parents kicked him out of the house for coming out as gay. "All That Can Wait" by Noriko Nakada imagines the consequences of misguided immigration policy on the community. "The Better Sister" by Tiara Ito is a gut-twisting journey that starts with two sisters in a tense relationship finding common ground.

This anthology includes introspection and unnerving private moments as well. "A False Start" by Catie Jarvis looks at the consequences of a momentous life decision. "The Makeup Lesson" by Sarah Haufrect follows a young woman on a visit to her estranged mother. "Drift, Longshore" by Karter Mycroft takes us to the beach and a strange encounter that readers won't soon forget.

And while many of the stories have a serious edge with some light moments of humor, the final story stands out for its over-the-top satire. "Soul-Searching in Topanga Canyon" by Laura McGhee is an amusing evisceration of new-age, self-help quackery, and it will leave you wanting more.

Our mission for the Made in L.A. fiction anthology series is to find and amplify the voices and stories of writers who see Los Angeles from many different perspectives. With this fifth installment, we're proud to include more writers from diverse communities than ever before, who tell stories that examine the intricate tapestry of lives in the region.

We hope you enjoy these stories for their heart, humor, and humanity and for the picture they paint from varied vantage points.

With our best wishes,

Made in L.A. Writers

Sara Chisolm ✶ Gabi Lorino ✶ Allison Rose ✶ Cody Sisco

THE COUCH

CHRISTINA HOAG

The mobile phone blared its over-loud, over-cheery tune. Desi bolted upright in bed and bashed her head on the top bunk. She seized the phone and slid the button to answer, more to silence the ringtone than to reply to the call. It was getting hard, this clandestine living in the police station.

It was the watch commander. "Desi, you're up to bat. We got a stiff in an alley: eleven-thousand block, behind Santa Monica. Sanitation guys called it in."

Desi rubbed her already throbbing skull. "What's it look like?"

"Male, white, twenties. Likely OD. It's three blocks from the station."

"Roger that."

Desi swung her legs off the thin mattress and checked the time: 5:11 a.m. *Shit.* She'd forgotten to set the alarm again. She had to be out of the cot room before Day Watch started arriving. She made the bed, plumped the pillow, and surveyed the room, making sure she'd left no trace of herself. She stuffed her backpack, containing clean underclothes, T-shirts, and sweats, under the bunk, pushing it into the farthest corner, and then cracked open the door. Seeing the hallway was clear, she dashed into the women's locker room.

Twenty-eight minutes later, hair dripping like a leaky faucet down the gully of her back, she ducked under the yellow tape that cordoned off the alley behind an eclectic collection of storefront businesses on Santa Monica Boulevard — a Mexican taco joint, a Thai massage parlor, a Vietnamese nail salon, and a hipster coffee shop.

"Nimmo, West L.A. Homicide," she announced to the blue suit, who jotted the information onto the scene log.

Another patrol officer milled around an abandoned corduroy couch, upon which lay a young man, cold and lifeless.

"Coroner?" Desi said.

"They're heading over," the officer said. "The sanitation crew had to continue their round, but I got their contact info in case you need it. How's Ray doing, by the way?"

"Good," Desi lied, stepping away from the officer to discourage chitchat. She was asked that almost every day, it seemed. She couldn't let it slip that she'd left Ray. Cops being the gossips that they were, it would be all over the department inside twenty-four hours, and she'd be persona non grata for leaving a hero, a cop's cop who'd been shot in the back by a fleeing drug dealer during a raid. The asshole was still in the wind, while Ray was marooned in a wheelchair.

She sized up the deceased. He boasted a tan and a messy man bun with what was likely a carefully calibrated stubble over his cheeks. He was better dressed than the typical street OD — a paisley button-down shirt worn loose over neat jeans, rolled up sleeves, docksiders with no socks — but this was Los Angeles' affluent Westside. She ran her eyes over his hands. No rings. A white band on his wrist indicating he usually wore a watch. At a glance, there appeared no sign of blood or injury indicating foul play.

She couldn't do much until the coroner's techs arrived. The dead were their domain. She turned to the patrol officer. "Get a search going for any hypos and shit. You know the drill."

Over the officer's shoulder at the far end of the alley, she clocked a familiar scruffy figure with a balding pate and a curtain of long gray hair floating around the shoulders of his tattered raincoat. In the invisible world of homeless street territory, this was his turf. He might have seen something last night.

"Sal!" she called.

He caught her gaze and scurried off, but she knew he wouldn't go far.

She strode around her end of the alley onto the boulevard, sweeping the block with her eyes. In the gap under a bus shelter wall, she spied a pair of fraying sneakers, the toe of one flapping free from the sole. She walked up to the structure. Sure enough, Sal was sitting on the bench. She stood at an angle to block his exit on the two open sides.

"Hey, Sal."

He answered with a frown.

She caught a noseful of human stink. He obviously hadn't been to the rescue mission in a while. She switched to breathing through her mouth as she patted her jacket pocket for the VapoRub she usually carried for death scenes and interactions with the homeless, but it was empty. *Shit, it must've fallen out in the rush of fleeing the house.*

"Did you see the guy on the couch in the alley last night?"

He stared at the gutter. A lie was coming. "Nope."

"Sal, remember how I saved your suitcase when you left it chained to this very bus shelter and a rook called out the bomb squad? You owe me one."

He scratched his chin through a thick matted beard. "He was on my couch."

"Dead or alive?"

"He was dead when I got there. The sonofabitch died on my couch. And I didn't roll him."

"Was he alone?"

"Far as I could tell."

"What time was this?"

"Nighttime."

"Late? Early?"

He shrugged.

She wasn't going to get any more out of him. "All right, then." She stepped away.

"Hey, Desi, you ain't gonna take the couch, are you?" The plaintiveness in his voice made her pivot. "The lady in the coffee shop said she don't mind if I sleep on it. She said I could use it as long as I wanted, and she wouldn't call for it to be picked up."

"Sal, you know the rules. Furniture isn't allowed in alleys. Sanitation found the body, so they probably already called bulk-waste pickup."

"Can you do something? I had to fight a couple guys over that couch. I'll get that watch for you."

He'd taken the watch. Of course, he had.

"I'll see what I can do." She walked off.

"You're a cop! You can do what you damn well please!" he yelled.

The words hit her like blows on the back. She felt a pinch of sympathy but quickly stifled it. If you let it, this job would chew you up and spit you out. She couldn't save the world.

When she got back to the dead man, the coroner's tech assistants were loading him into their van.

"Hey Desi, I was wondering where you were." Preeta, the forensic tech, hooked a stray hank of dark hair around her ear.

"Chasing a potential witness." She pointed with her chin at the body. "OD?"

Preeta whipped back the sheet to expose the dead man's bare feet. Small bruises bunched around his toes like spoiled grapes. "Third one this week on the Westside. Looks like there's some bad shit on the street. You might want to alert your narc guys."

"Will do."

She watched Preeta replace the sheet and close the van doors. Another life wasted by drugs.

"Catch you on the next one, Des."

She raised a hand in response and gave the all-clear to the patrol officers so they could resume their watch. Then a rumble behind her gave her a jolt. A massive blue truck appeared. *That was fast. It must've been in the neighborhood.* She darted out of its way as it extended its giant claw to grasp the couch, lifting it, and swinging it around to deposit in the rear bin with a dull thud.

The truck moved off with an engine snort, revealing Sal standing in the middle of the alley. He glowered at her. There was nothing she could do. He knew city ordinances better than most people.

She walked back to the station to get started on the report, stopping in the break room on her way to the detectives' bureau. She hadn't eaten breakfast, and her stomach felt like a bottomless pit. She fixed a cup of coffee and grabbed two strawberry Pop-Tarts, then entered the detectives' area, greeting several colleagues en route to her cubicle but not hovering to chat. She didn't want to talk to anyone. She sat at her desk and powered on the computer.

Finbar McNab reversed out of his cubicle on his wheeled chair. "Early morning jog again?"

"Huh?" *What was he talking about?*

"The other day. You were in super early with wet hair. You said you'd been running."

"Oh. No. Had a callout. OD in an alley."

He studied her for a second. "Everything all right? You don't look so hot."

"Thanks for the compliment."

"You've been putting in long hours lately, Des."

"Catching up on paperwork, parole board letters; you know how it is."

The truth was, she stayed in the bureau or break room until the station emptied so it was safer to occupy the cot room. Plus, she had no money to go anywhere. Then she had to be up early to avoid the station's first wave of arrivals. *It must be nice to work a nine-to-five*, she thought suddenly. There was a certain comfort in structured days.

"How's Ray?" McNab said. "Don't worry, sooner or later, we'll get the asshole who did this."

"If you don't mind, I have a report to write."

McNab threw up his hands in mock surrender. "Whoa, just asking."

He rolled his chair forward and disappeared into his cubicle.

Finally.

Desi took a deep breath and pulled up a blank report form, but her focus was gone. What people didn't know was that her four-year-old marriage was faltering before Ray got shot. He'd grown increasingly distant, was barely interested in sex. She asked him point-blank if he was having an affair. He said no. She told him she wanted out unless he agreed to go to couples' counseling, but he refused. She was pondering her next move when she got the call from his captain to get to the hospital. She wondered whether he'd chased the dealer, ignoring department protocols, and hurdled a chain-link fence right into an alley ambush in some sort of weird death wish.

She'd stayed, of course. She couldn't very well leave him when he needed her the most. But since the shooting, he'd spent more time drunk than sober and found fault with everything she did. She still had her badge, and he didn't.

After yet another fight, the cause of which she couldn't recall now, her mouth had launched the words like missiles: "I'm leaving." Ray hadn't said a damn thing. He simply rolled out to his garage man-cave, where he kept a small fridge stocked with beer. As she packed her life into garbage bags, he blasted Black Sabbath, which he knew she hated. Desi had no plan for where to go, but the fact that Ray had offered no resistance made her all the more resolute. He thought she was bluffing. She'd show him.

As she stared at the report, its blanks waiting to be filled in, she realized she missed her husband — the one she'd married, not this new version — but she didn't know if the old Ray would, or could, ever return. She pushed the intrusive nostalgia back into its mental box and concentrated on the report powering through. When she'd finished, she went to the break room to reward herself with more coffee and Pop-Tarts.

Lieutenant Migdalia Machado stuck her head out of her door as Desi walked by. "Desi, gotta minute?"

Desi turned. "Sure." She trailed her boss into her office. Machado had probably seen the stiff in the alley on the incident log when she came in. *She probably wants the rundown.*

"Close the door and have a seat."

Shit. Maybe not.

Machado reached under her desk and pulled out Desi's backpack. Desi slumped as if a vacuum had sucked all the air out of her body.

"Is this yours?"

Desi nodded. "I just put it there for safekeeping."

"Have you been using the cot room as a crash pad?"

"No. Well …"

"Save it."

Machado picked up an envelope from her desk and drew out two long auburn hairs, dangling them in the air. "There's only one person in the station with this hair. I found them in one of the bunks and on the floor. This explains why you were napping in your car in the parking lot the other evening, why you've been here at all hours, why microwave dinners, mac-and-cheese boxes, canned soup, and Pop-Tarts have appeared in the break room with your name on them, although all I've ever seen you eat is organic Whole Foodsy stuff.

"Listen, I don't know what's going on at home, and it's none of my business, but you know that sleeping in the cot room is strictly against the rules if it's not for official police business."

Desi didn't have the energy to lie any longer. "I left Ray." She suddenly felt as if an anvil had lifted off her chest.

Machado blinked. "I figured as much. I'm sure he's not easy to be around these days." Her tone softened.

"Are you gonna write me up for this?" Desi had an unblemished record. Not one complaint, internal or external, in fourteen years on the job.

"I'll make a deal with you. I'll pretend this never happened if you find somewhere else to live *and* you follow up on this for me." Machado turned to her computer and started typing.

Desi decided to wait until she finished to ask her not to broadcast her marital woes.

"Don't worry. I won't tell anyone about you and Ray," Machado said, not taking her eyes off the monitor. *Was she telepathic?*

"I'd appreciate that," Desi said.

Where was she going to go? Her credit cards were maxed out, and her credit rating had plummeted. She and Ray were down to a single income, plus Ray's disability check, but one of his favorite hobbies these days was ordering useless stuff from Amazon. Boxes piled up at the door almost daily. Plus, she'd had to take out a loan to retrofit the house for a wheelchair. She didn't have any friends outside the department or nearby relatives where she could crash for a few days. She'd spent the first night on her own in a West Hollywood motel that cost a hundred bucks for a room, despite a stained bedspread and stale pot reek, then decided to move into the station.

She thought it would be relatively easy to live there, for a short while anyway, since the station was equipped with a cot room, showers, lockers, and a kitchenette. It would give Ray enough time to realize how much he needed her. He'd come to appreciate her, beg her to come back. Then she'd have leverage to get him into therapy and rehab. But she hadn't banked on how stressful it would be to invent excuses to be at the station at odd hours and how people would pick up on the smallest changes in habit. She was juggling so many lies she could barely keep track of them all. It had been five days, and she still hadn't had as much as a text from Ray. Her shoulders sagged.

Machado hit enter with a flourish and twisted back to Desi. "The captain got an email yesterday from Councilman Hounanian's office, which he passed on to me, which I just forwarded to you. Report back to me by end of watch. Close the door on your way out."

As Desi walked back to her desk, she called up her email on her phone. When the Westside councilman called the captain, it always meant some bullshit complaint from his constituents: graffiti, people living in RVs parked at the curb, loud parties. She skimmed through the forwarded email and rolled her eyes. This one was bullshittier than usual. No wonder the LT had palmed it off as part of a deal. She drew a deep breath. She'd handle this, then figure out where she'd sleep that night.

* * *

Desi looked around the living room at the expectant faces of eight older residents of the upscale Brentwood neighborhood who had complained to the councilman that their cats and dogs were disappearing. An elderly lady, a cloud of snowy hair framing a birdlike face, gave her a friendly smile, which Desi returned.

"Have a seat, Detective." Sarah Cohen, the host and group organizer, gestured toward the dining chair pulled around the coffee table for extra seating. "Can I get you coffee?"

"No thanks. I can't stay long. I have witnesses to interview on another case." A pre-emptive lie.

Desi sat in the indicated chair, and Sarah perched on an ottoman next to her.

The elderly woman nudged a plate of oatmeal-raisin cookies toward Desi, who smiled noncommittally.

"I understand your pets have gone missing," she prompted, flipping open her notebook. She still couldn't quite believe she was investigating this.

Sarah unfolded a square of paper on top of the ziggurat of landscape photography books in the middle of the table. "This is what's been going on."

It was a map of the neighborhood marked with eight numbers and a corresponding key listing the pets and dates they were last seen.

"Jim." Sarah pointed to a bearded man on the couch who looked familiar.

He obediently raised his hand and said, "I canvassed the area to see how many pets had gone missing. As you can see, the disappearances started four months ago. All expensive breeds."

Jim leaned forward, elbows on his knees. "There's a pattern that makes me think there's something deliberate about it. It started with cats, then small dogs, then bigger dogs. It's not random."

Desi studied the list to verify what Jim was saying, wondering if he was Jim Hendrie, the movie director. She'd answered a call about a prowler at his house back when she was a patrol officer. He'd aged, but he still had those ice-blue eyes. She cast her eyes around the circle. "Has anyone noticed any strangers hanging around the neighborhood? Any odd bowls of food or water?"

"There's a shabby Econoline van that parks on my street at night," the elderly lady said.

"That shabby van belongs to my son," said a man, whose too-perfect hairline belied the presence of implants.

"What time of day did the animals disappear?" Desi asked.

"Mostly night." Sarah looked around the group for confirmation.

Heads nodded.

"I let my dog out at night in the backyard to do his business, and he never came back," said a woman pushing large, black-rimmed glasses up her nose. "Mine's the Pekinese."

"No unusual barking?"

Heads shook.

"Not to sound alarmist, but what if someone's engaging in some kind of animal sacrifice cult?" Jim said. "Like Santería or vodou or something."

Desi sucked in her lips to keep from bursting into laughter. *Rich people were too much.* "Those types of rituals usually involve hens and goats."

"We're completely baffled as to why our neighborhood would be targeted," Sarah said. "It's really quite worrying. What will they try next: home invasions? We have a lot of elderly residents."

Desi closed her notepad. "There's been a cat and dog shortage since the pandemic. People emptied shelters for pets to keep them company at home, so animals are getting high prices right now. I'd say that's the motive. And once their scheme works the first time, the thieves come back, getting better and bolder with each theft.

"They probably chose this neighborhood for the simple reason that it offers easy access to Sunset Boulevard and the 405, and it's all single-family homes with open yards. I suggest checking Craigslist to see if any of your pets are being sold online. If you find any you think are yours, call me."

Sarah bobbed her head at her neighbors. "Good idea, everyone."

Desi took out a wad of business cards from her pocket and handed it to Sarah, who took one and passed it on. Desi added, "I'll request patrol to step up neighborhood checks, especially at night. Keep your pets inside or on a leash. Don't let them roam by themselves, even in your yard. Somebody could be luring the animals with food that contains tranquilizers. Take a couple good photos of them, too, for identification purposes."

"Do you want to take a look around the neighborhood?" Jim asked.

"Not necessary. I saw it when I drove in." Desi stood.

"That's it?" said the old lady. "No fingerprinting?"

"Nothing to fingerprint, ma'am," Desi said. "Even though we'll have extra patrols, the best leads will come from residents. Stay alert. If you notice anything unusual, call me."

Sarah accompanied her to the front door and stepped outside onto the stoop with her. "Thank you so much for coming, Detective. I know you must have bigger crimes to handle, but for some people, their animals are all they've got. They're really bereft."

"I understand." Desi's eyes fixed on a burgundy tufted velvet couch across the street on the curb. She must've missed it on her way in as she was peering at house numbers. "Get back to me if you find anything."

She started walking across the street, but then it hit her. The couch. She and Sal were exactly the same. Homeless. Transgressors of rules. She turned. "Is someone throwing out that sofa?"

"That's Jim Hendrie's. The Salvation Army's coming to pick it up."

He *was* the film director. "Can you tell Jim to cancel the Salvation Army?"

Desi slid into the driver's seat of the Crown Vic and took out her phone. "Hey Fin, I need to borrow you and your pickup truck at lunchtime. I'll buy the sandwiches."

✳ ✳ ✳

A couple hours later, Desi wandered through the book stacks to the section of the West LA Regional Library with the internet-access computers. She spotted Sal right away. Having stopped at the drugstore on her way over, she daubed her nostrils with VapoRub before heading in his direction.

"Sal," she stage-whispered.

He looked around and pursed his lips in distaste when he saw her, then turned back to the monitor.

"I got a surprise for you. In the alley."

"What — steel bracelets with a nice little chain? Or a card that says, 'Go directly to jail. Do not pass go. Do not collect $200'?"

"Just come check it out."

"If I get up now, I'll lose my spot for the day."

"Suit yourself."

Desi walked out of the library onto Santa Monica Boulevard and past the station, heading to the coffee shop that backed onto Sal's alley. She managed to snare a free latte by casually pulling back her jacket to expose her gold detective shield, and then she waited in the alcove of the rear door to the alley.

Several minutes later, Sal turned the corner. She ducked back into the alcove so he wouldn't see her, then peered around the wall to keep him in view. She needn't have worried. He'd spotted the couch and barreled toward it like a torpedo. He stopped in front of it and stroked the velvet as if it would purr, then flopped on it with gusto, hands clasped behind his head.

Desi smiled. She'd done something right that day, at least. She pushed open the coffee shop door, walked through, and exited onto the street. Now Sal was sorted, she had to figure out where she was going to sleep. *Keisha.* Maybe she could ask her if she could crash on her couch for a night or two. As West L.A.'s only two female detectives, they'd been close before Keisha transferred to Pacific

Division. In all the drama with Ray, Desi had forgotten that she had a friend. As she walked back to the station, her cell phone buzzed in her pocket. She pulled it out and checked the caller ID.

It was Ray.

COME AS YOU ARE

RYAN SHOEMAKER

Author's note: This is a work of fiction. The roles played by Kurt Cobain, other characters, and any and all representations of public figures in this narrative are entirely fictional. While the facts surrounding Cobain's final week are well documented, all of Cobain's imagined actions and dialogue during this period of the narrative have no factual basis.

> "Bruises on the fruit, tender age in bloom."
> — Kurt Cobain, "In Bloom"

> "He walked out the back door of Exodus and climbed the six-foot wall … over the next two days, there were scattered sightings of Kurt."
> — Charles R. Cross, *Heavier Than Heaven: A Biography of Kurt Cobain*

Thursday, March 31, 1994, my eighteenth birthday. That was the day Scotty and I helped Kurt Cobain out of a tight spot and then jammed with him in my basement. I know what you're thinking — I'd have thought the same if it hadn't happened to me. But it did. This was back when I played guitar and Scotty drummed, back when we had this crazy idea, like a million other kids drunk on the grunge zeitgeist, that all we needed to be rock stars were some ratty jeans, a thrift-store cardigan, three guitar chords, and enough repressed angst to pen the next great teenage anthem. But that was years ago, six days before Kurt put a shotgun in his mouth, before Scotty really did become a rock star, and before I stopped caring about all of it. That day I met Kurt, that changed everything.

* * *

It happened like this. There we were at Tower Records on Sunset Strip, Scotty and me, free from Burbank for a couple hours. Soundgarden's "Spoonman" pounded through the sound system, Chris Cornell's raw-edged screech lifting our spirits as much as any Mormon hymn we'd sing at church on Sunday. And all those albums spread out before us!

My fingers flew through the CDs. Alice in Chains. The Melvins. Mudhoney. Nirvana. Pearl Jam. "Someday," I whispered to Scotty, "our album will be right here."

Scotty took a breath that could have sucked all the air out of Tower Records. "Yeah," he said. "Right here. Our album."

And then we heard this slurred voice rise above Chris Cornell's vocal blast. A wasted butt rocker, a relic from another era, in a denim jacket and tight, acid-washed jeans, was ragging Shaun, the cashier, about the music.

"Man, all you play now is this grunge shit," the guy griped. "What happened to Mötley Crüe, man? What happened to White Snake and Twisted Sister?"

"What happened?" Shaun said, throwing us a wink. "They're all in rehab, dude. They're all fat. They're done. Look for the reunion tour at the county fair."

Scotty and I laughed at that, what a lame-o, all while sneaking a glance at the cute hippie girl down the aisle from us in a black Pearl Jam T-shirt and Birkenstocks. Golden hair parted down the middle, ten perfect toes painted a bright aquamarine.

Then this other girl showed up, a round blush on her cheekbones, panting as she said to Pearl Jam Girl: "Callie, listen. This guy who works here said he just saw Kurt Cobain. Swear to God. The guy said Kurt just left, like a second ago."

Pearl Jam Girl grabbed her friend's elbow, dropped the CD in her hand, and they both shot out the door onto Sunset Blvd, their heads twisting east and west. Then, maybe, I saw a mess of long, ratty blond hair float past the far window and round the corner of the building. The girls must have seen it, too, because they screamed and ran.

Scotty eyed the door, his dark eyebrows rising like they were on strings. "You think?" he said.

We had heard the rumor that Kurt Cobain, at that very moment, was in a Los Angeles drug rehab.

I grabbed a Melvins album. On the cover, a couple of creepy cartoon kids smiled and fawned over a two-headed puppy. Sure, I felt the itch, too, to rush from the store, to hunt the parking lot and alleys — because perhaps it was Kurt Cobain. Just to see him, just to bask in his rebel aura and get his autograph, would be the chance of a lifetime. But it seemed so desperate, so pathetic, so uncool. "No," I said. "There's no way it's him."

✳   ✳   ✳

Fifteen minutes later we were back in my Ford Taurus station wagon, my mom's old car, squinting at the blurred figure on the cover of Soundgarden's *Superunknown*, my newest purchase. The silver Casio on my left wrist chimed. We didn't want to leave. But my dad would be pissed if I wasn't home by six thirty. He'd promised pizza from Tony's Bella Vista and a Porto's mango cheesecake for my birthday.

I turned the key and then cranked up the A/C. The car's interior had a tropical humidity, with a hint of mildew from a pile of damp blankets in the back seat we'd thrown on the grass a couple weeks ago at Valhalla Memorial Cemetery. A goth girl from AP English, Kami Boswell, claimed that at midnight on a full moon the spirits of the dead roamed the cemetery. She swore that she'd seen her grandmother there. I didn't believe her, or hardly believed her, but I had to try.

"You smell that?" I asked Scotty, catching a whiff of cigarettes in the car. And then from the backseat, there was the rustle of fabric and a low thump against the passenger side door. I caught Scotty's eyes as I turned to look, an electric tingle blitzing across my neck. The scuffed toe of a black, low-cut Converse poked out from under a blanket, and one blue, blood-shot eye glared at me through a gap in the folds. I was ready to bolt from the car, my mind filled with dangerous characters.

But then Pearl Jam Girl appeared at the passenger door and pounded a fist against the window. She panted, her part crooked, a hundred loose hairs lit by the sun. Moist stains bloomed under her armpits.

A muffled voice leaked from the blankets: "Don't tell them I'm here. Please." That voice! Unmistakable. A voice we'd heard a thousand times in MTV interviews, its cool, monotone bravado railing against the music establishment and sell-out bands, a voice that turned to gravel when screamed through a microphone.

Scotty cranked the window down. Pearl Jam Girl leaned in, her eyes wild, her breath coming in gasps. I could smell it, something like ammonia and saltine crackers. Her friend stood behind her, scanning the parking lot and bouncing up and down like she had to take a huge piss.

"Kurt Cobain," Pearl Jam Girl gulped. She had tears in her eyes. "He just ran by here. You see him?"

Scotty looked at me. For a second his eyes angled toward the pile of blankets. "No, didn't see anyone." He tipped his head until it touched the seat rest. "You see Kurt Cobain run by?" he asked me.

Pearl Jam Girl looked at me.

I tapped a finger against my chin, a casual gesture, an authentic gesture, to suggest I knew nothing. "I wish —"

Pearl Jam Girl didn't stick around to let me finish the sentence. She and her friend were racing back through the parking lot toward Sunset Blvd, little wedgies from their jean shorts riding up their butts.

Scotty and I just stared through the windshield, not wanting to turn around, as if this whole crazy, unbelievable moment — Kurt Cobain hiding in the backseat of my car — might vanish. And then that voice again, pleading: "Get me out of here."

I shifted the car into drive and inched through the parking lot, stopping to wait for a break in the traffic on Sunset Blvd. Pearl Jam Girl and her friend were on the sidewalk, cheeks wet with tears. We could hear them through Scotty's open window, inconsolable as they gushed to four other girls, the contagion of mania. I recognized that hysteria. I'd seen it in the old black-and-white newsreels of rabid teenyboppers ready to tear John, Paul, George, and Ringo limb from limb. I felt a sudden righteous zeal, a clear-eyed vision: saving Kurt from them, carrying him to safety.

As we idled there, the traffic rushing past, the seconds ticking by, Kurt, in an explosive rush of air and movement, threw the blankets off. Scotty and I flinched. Kurt was at the window, rolling it down. The girls looked at him with dumb doe eyes and then with a recognition that settled in their jaws like a heavy weight, pulling their mouths open to show all those perfect teeth. They screamed, a deafening industrial shriek, bodies convulsing, fingers pressed to their faces.

"Hey," Kurt said, half his body out the window. That shut them up as they waited for him to say something. Instead, a low, fleshy sound churned in Kurt's throat. His lips and nose quivered for a half second. Then a spray of yellow mucus shot from his mouth and splattered the girls. Kurt flipped them two stiff middle fingers. "Pearl Jam suck!" he yelled.

I stomped on the gas and squealed onto Sunset, hunched forward, hands knotted to the steering wheel. I didn't look back. I didn't want to see those girls' stunned faces.

Kurt took a huge breath, like a free diver surfacing from deep water. His forehead was slick with sweat. "Fucking parasites," he said.

I gave a casual shake of the head, like I agreed, though my heart smashed against my T-shirt so hard I thought Scotty might see it. "It's cool," I said, as if this were nothing; another day, another rock star saved from an adoring mob. But my thoughts were troubled by that image of Kurt, his sudden anger, his cruelty to those girls.

"No worries," Scotty said. A nervous vibrato rattled his voice.

Kurt laughed, a slow, easy chuckle that shattered the strangeness of the moment, a laugh dripping with sarcasm that eased my dark thoughts.

"I'm Toby," I said. "This is Scotty."

Scotty turned to look at Kurt. "We're in a band. I drum. Toby plays guitar. He's a lefty like you."

I cringed, as if Kurt Cobain cared about our band or that I was a lefty. We didn't even have a bassist.

"You play any shows yet?" Kurt asked.

The heavy traffic crawled along on Sunset Boulevard. A woman in a black bra and lacy underwear, nine stories high, gazed seductively down at us from the side of a glass and steel apartment building.

"One." And then I hesitated to add: "Some high school battle of the bands thing."

Kurt leaned forward. He looked awful, worn out. There were dark crescents under his eyes and scabby red blotches on his forehead and cheeks. The watch on his wrist, the dial a man's grinning face, caught the sun and cast a point of white light onto the car's ceiling. Above the watch was a white plastic wristband, the kind hospitals give patients.

"Was it awesome?" he asked.

I shrugged. "We just played two songs. We only have two songs."

Kurt licked his dry lips. "But was it awesome?"

Our two songs were me screaming into the microphone and playing amped up, sped up, shorter versions of whatever I was learning in *Guitar World*. But there was something special about playing, if only for our friends in their ripped jeans and oversize plaid shirts, as Principal Thorton tried to break up the mosh pit. Up on stage, the strike of those chords, Scotty's steady beat — there was a rush of euphoria. "Yeah," I admitted, "it was awesome."

Kurt reached into his shirt pocket, pulled out a cig- arette, and lit it. "Fuck yeah," he said, blowing smoke from the side of his mouth. "We once played in front of a grocery store, once in a RadioShack. Those were my favorite shows."

Smoke swirled through the car. Scotty and I looked at each other.

Kurt tapped the cigarette on the thin edge of the open window. "I need to get to North Hollywood."

* * *

We drove up Highland, past the Hollywood Bowl, and onto Barham. KROQ-FM oozed from the radio — the Gin Blossoms, Blind Melon, the Lemonheads — but the breezy silence sucked dry the music's electric cheer. Kurt sat there, hands crossed on his lap, a cigarette between his fingers.

"Shit," Kurt said suddenly, looking up at the Oakwood Apartments, a sprawling complex whose pitched rooflines seemed to hover over the tops of the thick trees edging Barham. "We used to live right there," he said, "that window on the corner. Dave and Krist and me. We recorded *Nevermind* just down the road." Kurt's lips curved into a pained grin. "There was this guy," Kurt said in a dry whisper that was almost lost in the rush of air through the open windows, "who lived a couple apartments down from us. Fucking annoying. Always knocking on our door, wanting to hang out, never shutting up about this kids' show he did in the seventies and how his parents stole all his money, and then some new, bullshit TV deal he was working on that would make him millions. All day he'd wander the hallways looking for someone to talk to. We wouldn't answer the door. We hid in the bushes if we saw him coming." Kurt stared at his hands. Smoke leaked from his nose. "That kids' show he did, I'd wake up early every Saturday to watch it. But I never told him that."

Wind whipped through the car's open windows bringing in the smell of eucalyptus and French fries and sewage. And then the San Fernando Valley opened before us, a brown haze pressing down on a tree-lined grid in full springtime bloom — a polluted Eden.

I couldn't believe the strangeness of all this, Scotty and me and Kurt Cobain. Yet Kurt was different; not the rock star from all the MTV interviews and music videos we salivated over. None of that aloof, anti-authoritarian hipness, none of the crazy antics with Krist and Dave, no hamming it up with fake French accents and silly faces.

"Fucking corporate radio," Kurt said, flicking his cigarette through the car window. "Why don't they ever play Mudhoney and the Melvins? And more fucking Nirvana?"

"Yeah," Scotty said. "More fucking Stone Temple Pilots, too."

In all the years we'd known each other, I'd never heard Scotty use the F word.

Kurt glared at him. "You're shitting me, right? Stone Temple Pilots? They're fucking boilerplate commercial rock, Nirvana rip-offs."

Scotty wilted, his shoulders shrinking, his head bending forward.

Kurt picked at a purple scab on his chin. His hand shook. "I need a fucking phone," he said.

We were coming up on Burbank Blvd and Hollywood Way. I made a quick right into a 7-Eleven. Kurt had the door open before the car even stopped. He walked to a payphone and yanked the handset from the cradle.

Kurt shouted into the phone, his fisted right hand hammering the air like a tyrant making a speech. He stared down at the sidewalk, his back curved, his lips moving quickly.

I turned the radio down to catch a word or phrase.

Then Kurt dropped the handset, leaving it to dangle above the sidewalk. He slid into the back seat and grabbed a folded piece of paper from his shirt pocket. "Laurel Canyon Boulevard and Saticoy. You know where that is?" he asked, squinting down at the paper.

"I think," I said.

I pulled onto Burbank Boulevard and drove west. Beck's "Loser" played on the radio, that buzzing sitar and final blast of distorted guitar over the repeating chorus, and then a second of silence before the first ringing notes of Nirvana's "All Apologies" filled the car.

"Hey," Scotty said, pointing at the radio. "Nirvana." He eyed Kurt like he'd pulled a rabbit from his ear. "How'd you do that?"

Kurt grinned. "When you're a big fucking rock star, you just make a call."

*　*　*

I turned right on Laurel Canyon and drove north, the car suddenly rattling over potholes and seams of patched, uneven asphalt. We passed through the twilight of a graffitied underpass crowded with shopping carts and shadowed figures, the reek of piss wafting through the car. Scotty fidgeted in his seat, his upper lip coated with sweat. This was a world we'd only caught glimpses of from the I-5 and the 170, a blur passing at seventy miles an hour.

"Here," Kurt said, pointing to a gray, white-trimmed apartment complex at the dead-end of Saticoy. One side bordered the 170, and though I couldn't see the traffic, the sound of it was like the steady rush of the ocean.

Kurt opened the car door and stepped out onto a patch of dirt dotted with dandelions and crabgrass.

"We can wait," I said. "It's no problem."

"Cool," Kurt said, but he was fixed on the building, like he could see through the white cinder block.

He walked to a rusted metal gate and pressed a button. Unable to stand still, those black Converse shuffled over the cracked sidewalk. The gate buzzed. Kurt pushed the door open, walked toward a dim hallway, and then vanished into darkness.

"You think it's true?" Scotty asked. "The drugs and all that?"

"That's the story," I said.

The hum of the freeway filled the car. Scotty stared at the spot where Kurt disappeared. "I thought he was in rehab."

"Maybe he was."

I thought of Rome. It'd been all over MTV for the last month: painkillers and champagne. Kurt in a coma. Some said Kurt was a junkie. Some said Rome was a suicide attempt. It made no sense. A rock star wife. A baby daughter. All that success. I didn't want to believe it. "What now?" I asked.

Scotty chewed his bottom lip, still looking at the dark hallway. "We take him to your house for dinner."

I laughed. "No way."

Scotty turned to me with a sly, crooked grin. "I'm serious. What a story we'll tell everyone on Monday."

"And my dad?" I said. "What would I say?"

Scotty had a look, something wild and hungry. "It'd be hilarious. Tell him that Kurt wants to be a Mormon."

I looked up at the building. Behind it, twilight filled the sky, a soft, luminous glow.

Several minutes later, the gate opened and crashed shut, and then Kurt was standing at the passenger window, drumming the roof of the car with his open palms, hips swaying, his silver wallet chain striking his belt buckle.

He leaned into the car, his elbows resting on the open window. "Hey, rock stars."

I didn't know what to say. Scotty looked at me and then jerked his head in Kurt's direction.

"So," I said, tracing the raised Ford logo on the steering wheel, "it's my birthday today."

Kurt gave a euphoric smile. "Hey, man, happy birthday."

"My dad's getting a pizza," I said. "Just him, Scotty, and me. No biggie, but you want to come? Or not. We can take you wherever you want."

"Yeah, cool," Kurt said, with a smile that looked ready to slide from his face, and pupils that were black specks in the center of those blue eyes.

* * *

By the time we got to Burbank, crickets were trilling from every front lawn and under every bush. A few points of starlight leaked through the golden-blue light of Hollywood that illuminated the pale night sky. I was late.

"Didn't I say six thirty?" my dad asked as we stepped into the entryway. A *Book of Mormon* open on his lap, he sat on the living room couch, still in the beige Carhartt work shirt he wore as the manager of a small factory in Van Nuys that made bumpers for cars.

"This is Kurt," I said.

Kurt stood between me and Scotty, hands clasped together in front of him. I wondered if my dad recognized him, but I saw nothing of recognition on his face, only concern as he absorbed Kurt's stringy hair and torn jeans, this strange adult with his son.

"Hi," my dad said, a little cold around the edges. He closed the *Book of Mormon*. "Toby, can I talk to you in the kitchen?" Kurt's eyebrows shot up and his eyes went wide, one of those you're-busted faces. My stomach jerked. I had this awful image of my dad throwing Kurt out of the house.

We stood in the semidarkness of the kitchen, facing each other, the refrigerator humming, the microwave blinking the wrong time. My dad's thick arms crossed in a perfect knot over his broad chest. "Who's Kurt?"

I explained Tower Records and that Kurt was in this cool band and how he needed a ride, and because it was my birthday, I thought it would be nice to invite him over. And then I played Scotty's card: "And I think he wants to be a Mormon. Not that he came right out and said it, but maybe he's a little lost, like, spiritually." And I said it with a straight face, a gloomy note in my voice.

"Really?" My dad's head swung toward the lit entryway, where Kurt and Scotty stood. For the past six months, since my mom died, my dad had thrown himself into church, a newfound devotion, mumbling scriptures as he walked through the house, devouring thick religious texts by long-dead Mormon prophets. Now he was a ward missionary and greeter, grinning madly and shaking hands each Sunday at the chapel doors.

I felt bad about the deception, but then looking from the dark kitchen to where Kurt stood, at his pale, blotchy face, I felt something unexpected claw my throat.

And then we were all at the table, a Tony's Bella Vista pizza box open between us.

My dad wiped his mouth with a napkin and then looked over at Kurt. "Kurt, Toby tells me you're in a band."

Kurt laid his half-eaten pizza slice on the paper plate in front of him. "Yes, sir." There was a formality in his voice, in his gestures, in the way he dabbed at the corners of his mouth with his napkin. "It's kind of a loud, high-energy rock band," he said. "I play guitar and sing. We're really hoping to make it big."

My dad leaned forward on his elbows. "And it's full time? It's your job?"

Scotty let out a little snort, then clamped his hand over his mouth. My dad looked at him, puzzled, and then back to Kurt.

Kurt stared thoughtfully at the pizza's wilted pepperoni. "Yeah, full time. Me and the guys. Nose to the grindstone and all that. We want to be famous. But if rock doesn't work, we'll try country. If not country, maybe reggae or opera or Inuit throat singing. And if that's a bust, I'll give up music for something stable, like being a sushi chef or maybe a garbage man or a logger."

"I see," my dad said, though I could tell he didn't know what to make of Kurt. Then: "Toby says you're interested in Mormonism."

Kurt looked at me, a narrow-eyed, I-got-this-dude look. Nine years between us, more than half my life, but a complete adolescent understanding of teenage lies and half-truths passed like telepathy across the table. "Yeah," Kurt said. "Totally. Like to be born again and all that, but with the Mormon Jesus, and the bread and the wine and the fish and the loaves."

My dad's lips opened, but Kurt went on, his right hand stroking the stubble on his dimpled chin: "I think I had a Mormon friend in junior high, or maybe he was Amish or Quaker. I can't remember. But what totally interests me about your church is all the wives, not that my friend's family was into that — only one mom — but that life really appeals to me: all the wives and kids. I've always wanted a big family. And don't you believe that you can become gods with all these superpowers?"

"Well, yes," my dad said, "but —"

"I'm totally behind it," Kurt said, "the long beard and the white robe, a throne with all my wives and kids around me. So cool." Kurt took a bite of pizza, chewing and speaking. "But not celebrating birthdays or Valentine's Day or Arbor Day? I don't know if I can commit to that."

"Kurt," my dad said, gripping the edge of the table with both hands, "the Mormon church doesn't practice polygamy anymore. That was almost a hundred years ago."

Kurt chewed his pizza and considered this. "You think they'll bring it back? I know a lot of guys who would join your church if they could have a few wives."

My dad's shoulders sank. The righteous zeal drained from his face. "Probably not, Kurt," he said.

Silence. Then Kurt's eyes drifted up to a painting that hung on the wall next to the table, a still life of a terracotta pot bursting with yellow poppies. It'd been there as long as I could remember, a relic from another life, a hobby my mom had, a distraction, she used to say, from her broken mind. Almost every wall in the house had one of her paintings: bowls of oranges and speckled red apples, vases spilling over with white tulips and pink carnations as big as my hands. I couldn't look at them.

"I like that painting," Kurt said.

My dad's jaw clenched. He gazed across the table, in my direction, but I knew he couldn't see me but something from long ago. "My wife painted it," he said. "Toby's mom." He smiled, a smile from another time. "Painting. She called it her therapy." My dad stared down at his plate. "She passed away in October."

As if something had called to me, I turned from the table to look into the dim living room where six circles, the size of half dollars, were pressed into the beige carpet. I'd tried to smooth them out with my hand, comb them out, run a vacuum over them, but they stayed: the imprints of the hospital bed where my mom lay for the last two weeks of her life.

I'd read something in my ninth-grade English class about how the mind's a dark forest. I guess that's how I made sense of it: that my mom got lost somewhere in her mind and couldn't find her way out. Worn down and scared for so many years, she just gave up and let herself waste away, even as my dad and I pleaded with her to take some water and a little soup — because that's all she needed to save her body. But she wouldn't.

It's hard to say "suicide," but I should probably call it what it is, even if there wasn't a bullet or a handful of pills or a crushing fall, and even if it took years of hospitals, psychiatrists, LA County social workers coming and going. There would be long stretches when she seemed like a normal mom, but always the eventual backslide, each time a little deeper into that forest until she wandered off, farther than she ever had, and never came out.

And where did all her pain go? As far as I could tell, she left it behind for me and my dad. I guess that's why I'd tried not to think about her.

I looked at Kurt. He had one elbow on the table, his chin on his palm, that white plastic bracelet touching the tattered edge of his shirtsleeve. He'd followed my gaze to the carpet, and then he smiled, like he could see right into me.

And that look never left Kurt's face as he sang "Happy Birthday" along with my dad and Scotty and as I blew out the candles and my dad dropped huge slices of mango cheesecake onto our plates. And that smile was still there when we finished the cake, when Kurt said, "We should jam together."

I felt a rush hit my brain. "Can we?" I asked my dad.

I looked at Scotty. He was practically panting.

"I don't know." My dad frowned at his watch. "It's a school night."

But then I played another card. "I thought maybe on my birthday it would be all right. Just this once."

My dad's arms flopped to his side. "Okay," he said. "But not too late."

∗　∗　∗

We led Kurt down a narrow staircase to a room in the basement where we stored our Christmas decorations. All our equipment was down there: Scotty's drum kit, my Fender Squire and Epiphone acoustic, two Peavey amps, and a mic duct-taped to a wobbly stand we found at Goodwill.

"This is it," I said, knowing Kurt might appreciate the yellow linoleum and the bleak bone-white of the overhead fluorescent lighting, all in hilarious contrast to the fake Christmas tree and 40-inch plastic Santa Claus in the far corner of the room.

Kurt raised up onto his tiptoes and poked a water-stained ceiling tile. "The shittier the better," he said.

I lifted my Fender Squier and held it out to Kurt, hoping that something of him might absorb into the guitar. "You working on anything?" I couldn't help asking.

Kurt reached for the guitar and eased the strap over his shoulder. I flipped the amps on.

"That's what everyone wants to know," Kurt said into the microphone, his amplified voice filling the room. "There's some rumor about a blues album, but that's bull-shit. You want to know something?" Kurt twisted the guitar's tuning pegs, smirking with some secret knowledge. "Truth is, I've written one song in the last six months, one depressing little piece of shit." Upstairs, a toilet flushed. Water rushed through a pipe somewhere above the stained ceiling tiles. "You want to hear it?" he asked, not looking at us, like he thought we might turn him down.

Scotty and I nodded dumbly in unison, feeling stupid and pathetic, like we'd synchronized it.

Kurt started strumming, a fast up and down in a minor key that sent a sudden shiver across my chest and down my back, that eerie feeling of peering into empty rooms or at old grainy photos. I leaned in, hoping for a key change, for Kurt to tap the fuzz pedal and lift the song from its sad groove. I waited for the stinging lyrics, something quintessentially Nirvana, the shocking, incongruous images, the railing social commentary against the phonies and the wannabes.

Then Kurt stepped up to the mic, his voice groaning out of him, like a deep ache as he sang, something about a son who'd tried again and again to make his parents proud. I looked at Scotty, his faded navy Vans tapping time with the downbeat, his smile until, absorbing the words, his foot slowed and then stopped. He slumped into one of the lawn chairs we kept in the room and stared down at the pattern of dizzying loops and swirls in the yellow linoleum. And I was hunched over in one of the lawn chairs, too, though I couldn't remember sitting. My right hand covered my mouth.

Kurt let the final chord ring until the strings stopped vibrating. Scotty swallowed hard and then stood up. He looked at me and then back to Kurt.

"Next album?" is all Scotty could say.

Kurt ran his hand across the short stubble on his cheeks. He didn't look at us, but at something above our heads. "No, that one's just for me."

The three of us stood there. The amps buzzed. Kurt shook his head. "Fuck," he said. "It's your birthday." He struck a major chord. "Let's play something."

Scotty didn't hesitate, reaching his drum kit in three long steps. I was at my Epiphone acoustic in two, throwing the strap over my shoulder. And when I brushed my pick over the strings and they sounded right, I looked at Scotty, his two raised fists ready to lay into the snare drum and hi-hats.

"How about 'Smoke on the Water'?" Kurt said. "Or 'Wild Thing'?"

"How about 'Teen Spirit'?" I said.

Kurt groaned. "Oh, God, aren't you sick of that fucking song?" He looked over at Scotty and then at me. Scotty's hair was wild, his eyes swelling from the sockets. I must have looked about the same.

Kurt smiled. "You two look fucking pathetic." He played an F minor, the song's first unmistakable chord. "You know it?" Kurt asked, and I laughed at that because not to know it — not to have strummed along a thousand times with Kurt as his voice wailed from the speakers in my room — would have been unforgivable to anyone at school who played guitar.

A thin blush rose through Kurt's patchy scruff. "Okay," he said. And then he counted to three, and together we played those first four chords, and it was like hearing the song for the first time, when its gravity pulled me toward the radio, a sound I'd never heard before, the wrecking ball that toppled all those stupid eighties hair bands. A clean electric sound filled the room until Kurt tapped the fuzz pedal with his right foot and a booming static erupted from the amp. That's when Scotty, right on cue, laid into the snare drum. And I was right there with Kurt, my left hand a blur against the bronze strings and black pickguard. I looked at Kurt and, in an instant, he'd become what I wanted him to be. Not that pissed off, worn-out rock star chain smoking in the back of my car but the Kurt Cobain

I'd meticulously studied in all that MTV concert footage, that slight straddle, his whole body swaying forward and back, soaked through with the pure thrill of the music. And right before Kurt stepped to the mic and I lost his face behind that curtain of blond hair, he looked at me and smiled, a benevolent, big-hearted smile.

✳ ✳ ✳

It was past eleven when we drove Kurt — conked out in the backseat, head against the window, arms hugging his body — to LAX. I didn't want the radio on. Whatever KROQ was pumping out at that hour would only dilute the raw sound looping through my brain, Kurt's voice, its energy. I wanted to savor it before time grabbed it away.

I looked at Scotty, an outline in the darkness momentarily illuminated by the towering lights above the 405, his lips moving but with no sound, this strange moment like a sweet, fleeting flavor on his tongue.

Kurt didn't stir as we pulled to the curb in front of the airport terminal. "Hey," Scotty whispered, shaking Kurt's knee. Kurt's eyes snapped open. He squinted up at the glaring terminal lights. A few stray hairs were smeared across his damp forehead, and two thin lines of snot leaked from his nostrils.

"Well," Kurt said, flashing that sly rock star smile, "you think anyone will believe you, the fucking night you hung out with Kurt Cobain?" He was fighting for that smile. Whatever he had surging through his veins earlier was almost used up.

Kurt pulled the crumpled directions to that cinder block apartment from his shirt pocket. "You got a pen?" He tore the paper into two ragged halves.

36

Scotty dove for the glove compartment, pushing through CD cases and wadded Kleenex, until he pulled out a dull pencil.

Kurt scratched his name on the two halves and handed them over the seat. Scotty held his, absorbed in tracing Kurt's signature with his finger.

Then Kurt unclipped the silver chain from his wallet and belt loop. "Happy birthday," he said.

The chain swung from Kurt's thumb, the same chain I'd seen bouncing on his hip in concert footage from The Paramount and Live and Loud. It seemed too personal, an extension of his body. I shook my head. "I can't."

"Take it." Kurt took my hand and dropped the chain into my damp palm.

I held it, hefting its cool weight, and before I could stop myself, I asked, "What about you?" I was really asking about the hotel room in Rome and the cinder block apartment and the plastic bracelet on Kurt's wrist. "We can take you back." I held my breath. My heart pounded. "If you want."

The skin around Kurt's eyes tightened, the briefest flash of annoyance, Kurt's rebel spirit rising. But then his eyes softened. "No, I'm a fucking hopeless case. Always have been," he said, opening the door and stepping onto the curb. He turned and leaned into the car. "Hey, your mom's paintings," he said, "they're pretty awesome. Beautiful. It's cool she left them for you."

And with that, Kurt walked into the terminal, the light there as bright as the noonday sun, and when I blinked, I saw Kurt's thin, white outline against the black backdrop of my closed eyelids before the image burned out.

"I'm framing this," Scotty said, stroking Kurt's signature with his fingertips.

I leaned forward until my head rested on the steering wheel. I thought of all my mom's paintings, and how I couldn't look at them without seeing her shrunken face against a white pillow. I suddenly knew Kurt was wrong. Where was the beauty there? I didn't see it.

I opened the car door and walked into the terminal. I heard Scotty through the open window. "Hey," he shouted. But I didn't turn. The terminal doors opened with a blast of warm air that shot down on me. I was moving quickly toward Kurt, my steps strangely loud in the near-empty terminal.

"Kurt," I said. He turned. I was suddenly self-conscious. He was no longer part of my world but had returned to his, the rock star on the cover of *Rolling Stone*, the subject of a thousand rumors, the rebel voice of a generation. Three screens above us, all those arrivals and departures, cast a yellow light onto the polished floor. A man and woman studying the rows of departing flights, not much older than Kurt, both in red flannel shirts, torn jeans, and Doc Marten boots, looked at us. A soft gasp squeaked through the woman's lips. She leaned toward the man and whispered in his ear.

"I'd rather have her than all those paintings," I told Kurt. My voice slipped. Something broke up and stirred in my chest, some old feeling. "All that pain she had," I said. "Maybe she didn't even realize it. Maybe she thought she'd take it with her. But it just stays behind."

Kurt didn't say anything. He didn't move, and his face at that moment — framed by his long, greasy hair, his eyes almost in shadow — is forever fixed in my mind. He looked at me, but I wasn't sure he saw me or something else, maybe some scene playing out in his mind. His stubbled chin dropped to his chest, and he twisted his head away from me until I couldn't see his face. Then he turned and walked away.

"Is that Kurt Cobain?" the woman asked. She wore a black Alice in Chains tour shirt under the unbuttoned flannel. The man stood at her side, licking his lips, waiting for me to say something. His red flannel shirt had an ironed crease running up each sleeve, and the black Doc Martens didn't have a scuff or mark on the leather, like they'd just come out of a box. In six months, in a year, they'd be wearing something else, listening to something else.

"Fuck off," I said, and walked away.

In the car, Scotty sat there, still mesmerized by Kurt's autograph. "I'm bringing this to school. I'm showing it to everyone." He raised the thin scrap of paper to his nose and sniffed its edges. "What'd you say to him?"

I gripped the steering wheel, the engine's idle vibrating through my arms.

Deep in my right pocket, I felt the weight of Kurt's wallet chain. "I don't think he's all right," I said. But Scotty didn't hear me. He was humming something, tapping his heels against the floor mats, still staring at Kurt's signature as I pulled away from the terminal curb.

The 405 and 101 swarmed with an absurd midnight traffic as we crawled toward Burbank. My dad would be pissed. So would Scotty's parents. I'd probably lose the car for a month. But I didn't care. As the exits ticked past, I tried clearing my throat a few times and looking over at Scotty. I wanted to talk about what happened, to make sense of it. But Scotty never looked up, his eyes fixed on Kurt's signature, never saying a word, even as I pulled into his driveway. He opened the car door, heaved it shut, and disappeared into the house.

That night a space opened between us until we drifted apart at the end of the summer, me to Brigham Young

University and soon after to a Mormon mission in Chicago, and Scotty to start a band with some guys from Burbank High. Within a couple years, they built a following around Los Angeles. KROQ featured them twice as a New Pick of the Week, and then they were playing the Whiskey and the Troubadour. And then they had a record deal, appearances on *The Late Show* and *Conan*, and last I heard they were opening for The Shins. But before all that, I don't think Scotty ever forgave me for that Friday morning he showed up to school with Kurt's autograph in a cheap black plastic frame and a story so incredible that our friends laughed to tears, but I didn't back him up. I never talked about it then — because no one would have believed us, anyway. The truth is that something profound happened that night, yet its meaning that Friday morning hovered just beyond my reach, and to even bring it up felt wrong. But Scotty never understood that. All he saw from that night was a story.

✳ ✳ ✳

Sunday, April 10. I watched Kurt's memorial on MTV, five thousand kids at the Seattle Center lighting candles and wiping tears as Courtney Love read Kurt's suicide note.

I was in the kitchen Friday morning when I'd heard the news on KROQ's Kevin and Bean Show: "Shotgun wound to the head … body found at home … suicide note … untimely death." And when I heard it, I remember looking over at the table, at the cushioned chair Kurt had sat in, then up at the yellow poppies my mom had painted. A shiver slid down my spine. Then I was sitting on the kitchen floor, the tiles cold through my jeans. I sensed a familiar, sad anger in me. Once again, I was arriving at a line of demarcation in my life, something ending and something new and unknown beginning.

I was angry as Courtney read that note, at what Kurt had done to himself. I could hardly believe what she read, in Kurt's own words: how he couldn't feel the music anymore, his guilt for going through the motions night after night on stage. And hearing that, it was hard to be angry. I thought of Kurt in my basement, an image as vivid today as it was then, only six days from his end, strung out on heroin, hating life, hopeless, numb. Yet, with his eyes closed, hair damp with sweat, body thrashing with the music, Kurt's last performance: a gift.

When the memorial ended, I walked into the kitchen and turned on the radio. Green Day's "Longview," on heavy rotation for the last month, was ending, the bass line fading out. A window was open. Birds whistled in the backyard. Ecstatic voices barked from the radio: a new furniture store in Glendale; a sale at JCPenney; lower insurance rates for safe drivers. Any moment the music would start again — all those songs, the soundtrack of my teenage life. But I understood how, from that moment, they would never quite sound the same.

HALF-BURIED HEARTS

HAZEL KIGHT WITHAM

Mina and I met when we were stuck at school one day early in fourth grade because neither one of our parents signed and returned a field-trip form. For me, it was because I had just moved to the area after my mom vanished the year before, and nothing was quite right with Dad in our already over-stuffed apartment near LAX on the edge of Westchester, dangerously close to the "diverse" side of town. (He used a different word.) And paperwork was never his forte. For Mina, it was because her single mom was working round the clock to make tenure and raise a child. Both of them dropped the ball and had zero backup.

We had a strict, brittle man as our teacher that year, an anomaly in the world of female elementary school teachers. I liked Mr. Auercloch — pronounced "hour clock," as in his favorite catchphrase: "Stay on the Hour-Clock!" — in the way kidnap victims grow fond of their abductors as they settle in for the long haul. But Mina did not. And so, when we were the two kids left out of the science museum field trip, we spent the day being aloof fourth graders in Mrs. Healy's first grade class. She had been Mina's teacher, not mine, and according to Mina, Mrs. Healy was trusted to babysit her that day. Since I was more listener than talker, more silent subverter than overt jokester, the school assumed I'd be fine anywhere.

That was the day we became BFFs. We sat at the back of Mrs. Healy's room stapling student names onto their paint-splatters and then mounting said "art projects" onto black construction paper. I said to Mina I didn't understand why teachers spent so much time on the bulletin board game when all the artwork was going to end up in the trash can.

She leveled her no-fooling, you-got-to-be-kidding gaze at me and said, "Students like to see their efforts celebrated by their teachers. It makes all the work you put in worth it. Besides, you do not know anything about Mrs. Healy's Gratitude Art Show that she puts on before Thanksgiving each year, so hush it, white girl."

"*Okay* then, so-rree." I'm not so quick with the comebacks and fumbled in my brain for something I could call her, but I didn't think we were cool like that yet. I glue-sticked the back of some kid's orange and fuchsia catastrophe and aligned the edges to make the border even on the construction paper. Grinning, I said, "I'm so *grateful* to be part of the gratitude show I'll likely not get invited to."

Mina stone-colded me again. There was no cracking this girl. A beat later she said, "I'm so grateful I get to use my field trip day to support younger humans in their artistic endeavors."

Seriously, she talked like this at age ten.

Unable to mirror her coldness, I offered a luke-warm retort: "I'm so grateful I get to hang out with a girl who can't stand me and play teacher's assistant instead of watching Albert Zarias pick his nose and camo it against the vinyl bus seat."

A laugh burbled out of Mina's mouth before she could wrangle it back. Triumph swelled in my ten-year-old chest. I'd won! I cracked the stone-cold Mina Devereux! And then, trying to summon her icy stare, I doubled down: "I'm so glad I get to make construction paper frames for first graders instead of seeing how many times Ximena Alvarez tries to switch seats to spread chisme without the bus driver knowing." I felt great pride that I knew what chisme meant and could use it in a sentence.

She tried briefly to reel it all in but soon let go, her laugh unspooling in the air between us. I saw for the first time her face take shape into something beyond guarded. It was like I'd found a key that could unlock any door.

*   *   *

In the earliest years of our friendship, my biggest fear was Mina discovering my father was an unabashed racist.

"We stick to our own tribe," he liked to say, using a word appropriated from Native peoples and borrowing it to reinforce his segregationist beliefs.

But it was thanks to him I first learned about truth and reconciliation practices as a way toward racial healing. We watched *Invictus*, the movie with Morgan Freeman playing Nelson Mandela, who managed to rise up from imprisoned activist to visionary thinker to apartheid healer and become the first Black president of a segregated South Africa. My father thinks the thing you need to do to pretend you're not racist is to watch movies with Black people in them and call it a day.

Because there is some part of him that wants to play at being non-racist, he offered a steady diet of movies anchored by Morgan Freeman. *The Shawshank Redemption* was a favorite, *Driving Miss Daisy* for the sentimental days, and some Western … *Unforgiven*, I think. *Unsmiling* was more like it. Consequently, my summers were populated by people of color only through a screen at night after I had tagged along on my dad's work errands all day. The rest of my year was spent at school surrounded by a slew of folks my dad would never bother to notice other than to make petty comments about from inside the safety of his vehicle.

However, in my public elementary school at the border of a white neighborhood and a diverse one, I found another kind of family. I knew their names, their stories, their likes and dislikes, and they knew mine. To make up for the lack of diversity in our home and my father's racist comments, I cultivated actual friendships. Which is more than I can say for the bond between Morgan Freeman and Bascomb Slater, a.k.a., the big guy I called Dad.

* * *

I was first able to name my father's racist BS when I was seven, just after Mom's evaporation. I wore pin-striped maroon capris, that were tightening by the day, and dusty off-brand sneakers that never looked like the kicks other kids rocked. My dad and I were driving to some garage sales to score deals that he always saw as a grand accomplishment, like the God of Bargains was personally blessing him with a boatload of *Gunsmoke* VHS tapes or seventeen ski hats in various shades of puke, even though we lived in Southern California and never had money to go see snow, much less go skiing or snowboarding.

That year he said he'd take me to the mountains, but, at seven, I knew it was only a ploy in the games he was still committed to playing with my mom, even though she was no longer in the picture. (When Mom decided she'd had enough of Dad, she didn't have enough to break me out with her. For a while she would call and say she was working on it, but she was never quite able to. I didn't understand how little me could be such a bother, why she couldn't just take me. Five years later, I still didn't.)

So, one morning, my dad and I hit three different garage sales in Culver City before eight o'clock to gear up for snow, and I became the unenthused owner of an extra-large rust-brown puffy vest and an old avocado-green scarf that was pilling from overuse. I had no choice in either purchase, but imagined beaming tropical sunshine over the ski place we were supposedly going to visit so it would not be cold enough to warrant either wardrobe disaster.

Hunting for another yard sale, Dad had pulled his truck onto a street with a canopy of delicate green above us. As he slowed mid-block, where another yard sale sprawled its glory, I was momentarily enchanted by the early sun filtering through feathery leaves of the trees that lined the entire block, one in front of every house, wondering who organized such a precise planting.

One of my father's endearing qualities was the ability to identify any tree. It was a topic I could redirect him toward when a subject was in need of changing. So, I asked, "What kind of trees are these, Dad?"

He was feeling around for his wallet in the wooden clementines crate that lived between us on the bench seat among receipts, cherry Lifesavers, to-go ketchups, packets of hand wipes. He paused, looked up, and answered, "Chinese elms," but before an arboreal lecture could begin, someone honked behind us and I heard the frustrated voice of someone directing their energy at us.

My stomach dropped like an anvil in one of those ancient cartoons: my dad was never one to back down from a conflict. I looked into the side mirror, along the primer gray of our pickup, and saw an older man, Hispanic, a little stooped, getting out of a car behind us, one that was blocking the neighboring driveway. His shirt was clean-pressed, his neck glittered with a simple chain, his hands were open in bewilderment. I could tell he was upset over the parking nab that my father had executed.

My dad, out of the car already and heading to the lawn loot, tossed back an exaggerated, "Sorry, es-aay, first-come, first-served, capeesh?" My dad had no problem sprinkling various Spanish and Italian words at anyone he decided was Other and should be mindful that he could, therefore, dictate their "place."

The man cocked his head as my dad continued toward the garage sale, and with a simple, "Excuse me, sir," did something unthinkable. The politeness in the man's voice stopped my bull-in-a-china-shop father. My dad hesitated, then looked back.

My dad's face was contorted in a lemon squeeze of derision. All bluster and fake innocence, he asked, "What? Qué pasa?"

By the second use of Spanish, I was ready to flee. I wanted to be as far away as possible, anywhere. Just vanish. I was still inside the vehicle, melting into the seat.

The man spoke calmly, slowly; pretty much the opposite of my dad's style. "Sir, you took the spot I was about to pull into. I was backing my car up so that I could line up better when you came in."

My dad looked around to see if there was an audience, which there was — the other garage sale customers — and said, "Guess you didn't pay enough attention in Driver's Ed to get in on the first try. But maybe they don't do Driver's Ed where you come from. Won't be a minute."

He glanced at me. "Let's go, Tike!" My dad's term of endearment.

The man looked at me, and something in his resigned brown eyes told me I had a choice right then: I could obey my father, as was always expected, or I could take a small but important stand. His kind eyes told me he knew the choice I wanted to make. Instead, I shouldered open the door and slouched off to view the sorry array of objects splayed across the lawn. But I paused, looked back, and watched the man tip his hat to me, his smile as weary as his eyes. Then he said, "Qué será, será."

It struck me as strange, because that was the name of a song my dad used to sing to me when I was smaller, before turning off the light and kissing me goodnight, sandpaper stubble against my forehead. I stared at the man, who closed his eyes in a long blink then turned away, as the next line played in my head: *whatever will be, will be*, as the man headed back to his car.

✳   ✳   ✳

I sought to understand the ugliness that infiltrated my home courtesy of Bascomb Slater. After Mina and I bonded in early fourth grade, she was one of my best teachers of how history was still playing out in the present. She told me about the small cuts from tiny daggers that began as early as memory, and about being a Black girl in white spaces, in which she was trained to be vigilant. Her teacher, on the first day of kindergarten, had everyone put their hands on their desks to take in "our rainbow of skin tones." Mina refused, unwilling to display her dark skin against so much lightness. The teacher had singled her out even more than she'd already been, and Mina's chest burned at the small stand she was taking and the way the teacher would so readily trample that rebellion.

Her refusal turned that teacher against her, and that one interaction seemed to embitter the rest of their time that year. From then on, Mina always felt on the outside of a circle. Though there were other kids of color in the class, none were as dark as she, and none dared defy the teacher. The rest went along "like lambs," while Mina observed, watched.

She became schoolyard protector of kids excluded from two-touch or kickball, calling out to the captains, "How long before you pick someone who doesn't look like you?" Other kids called it mean. Mina called it justice.

She also had a litany of affectionate names for me that cut me down to size when I needed it. She said I hadn't endured enough micro-aggressions in my life and that my white skin was too thin, so she kept me in line by name-checking me often. Some of her favorites were "Luce," for translucent, a reference to my paleness; "Off-Brand," which refered to my lack of style, but which I contend was more my lack of resources; and "Biff," which was my favorite, because it was her way of calling me her BFF, a term of endearment to let me know that I was tolerable.

Mina acted as my moral compass, following the rules not necessarily because she wanted to but because she had to. As she often told me, especially in the wilds of middle school, my seemingly harmless rule-breaking, my small thrill-seeking mischiefs (such as entering through an exit, sneaking into a second movie, and pocketing a Brach's butterscotch), could land a Black girl like her in trouble with the authorities, or worse. My rule-breaking was an exercise of my white privilege that she, out of principle and self-preservation, had to avoid.

Her mother was a professor of Ethnic Studies at Cal State Long Beach and raised Mina on Nina Simone records, James Baldwin wisdoms, and a deep historical knowledge of brave activists. Her single mother didn't have family nearby, so she took young Mina with her to meetings and office hours, hushed her in a corner with a look and a pile of books for company, and went about the business of being a strong woman of color raising her child in an unfair world.

She knew the value of having a community that supports you, one that reflects you back to you. In their case, a strong community meant church, which made Sunday Mina's favorite day, not for the God-talk or the after-service snacks, but for the array of brilliant variation around her: so many Black folks, so many shades, all able to fit in the same space, all welcomed and held. But her mom also chose to drive a little farther to make sure Mina was in a school that was more resourced than the ones in their own neighborhood.

And so, Mina learned to remain calm in the face of meanness from both kids and adults. She taught me about stoicism: to be logical, reasonable, and strong against the vagaries of fortune. Mina kept herself in check, on an even keel, not attached to the acceptance of those in her school. But she also kept watch and was a playground vigilante when the mean kids tried to swing their might. She never involved the adults, never relied on them to arbitrate an adult's lopsided justice. Instead, she used her size — biggest and tallest in her grade and the one above — to maintain fairness as *she* saw it. Her outcast status gave her a kind of power. She only needed to saunter up to one of the alphas and give them that blank, unsmiling look that said, "You know what's right, and you're gonna do it."

Because her methods were usually without words or physical contact, the kids who buckled had no explicit complaint they could level against her. Her way won.

* * *

When we were in his truck driving around the city, my dad would heckle people he saw on the street who were doing something that deviated from his code of conduct. Or even just daring to exist. Women joggers with big breasts were told to "try a bra, lady." Asian drivers were called "Ornamentals." A Black man crossing the street was greeted with, "Hey jive cat, what's happ'nin'?" None of the targets ever heard my father say any of these things, but I did. They were his target, and I was his audience, trapped inside a vehicle forever powered by Dad's vitriol.

When describing a Latina nurse at the doctor's office, he would imitate her accent when retelling the story of him not understanding her, which I suspected was him just not listening. This was his default position, alongside a persistent belief that anyone white was right.

I knew my father was reducing people to ugly stereotypes and labels, even though I did not get explicit instruction in anything else. Maybe that is why, from the lack of love-thy-neighbor sentiment in our apartment and in his truck, I tried to take a stand where I could and make friends from different cultures.

And though I was brave in certain places, I was still fearful with him. I never told my dad about the friendship with Mina that blossomed that fourth-grade fall. When he would ask me who I wanted to invite over to play, I would say, "No one," in part because I was scared of what he would say to them, in part because I didn't want anyone to see our home and the objects that overwhelmed it, and in part — the largest part — because my favorite person to spend time with was a Black girl who called BS on everything he stood for.

* * *

And then one day in the fall of seventh grade, my dad caught me hanging with Mina after school.

We were out on the handball courts, blasting the ball as hard as we could back and forth, gripped fully in that pulsing rhythm, the kicky-smash against the concrete, the satisfying thwang against the muraled backstop of the liver-colored handball with its surface pattern of interlocking circles that I loved beyond reason.

Blessedly, Mina and I had ended up at the same school, Wright Middle, which was nestled in the nicer part of Westchester, near LAX. Mina called this area "Whitechester" because even though our school was properly mixed, the population of the neighborhood was not. She and I lived on either side of the border between white Westchester and Inglewood, an area that was very diverse, much to my father's chagrin.

At Wright, Mina was my true north as puberty set in and I tried to figure out how to coexist with the Mean Girls and Cool Boys. Acne rooted and sprouted across my pink skin, and my body began to blossom into something I had no blueprint for. Mom was still MIA, visible in only Christmas cards and birthday wishes, and so Mina and her mom subbed in.

In the catalog of middle school skills, I was good at handball. It was the one ball sport I could master, aside from tetherball, which always had the blessing of rope to keep that ball contained. But if I was good at handball, Mina was Lights Out. Her play style was a thing of wonder. It was similar to her personality: a combination of stillness and precision. She was able to wait before moving to where the ball was, and when she did move, it was with a breathtaking certainty, quickness, and power. I was always nervous and scattered and frantic across the court, wasting energy with my frazzle. However, I could get the ball places that were unexpected. I saw my strategy as utilizing the distraction method: opponents were trying to figure out what my body was up to while I was slamming the ball from a wackadoodle angle.

I was distracted that late October day when I had skipped the ride home I usually took with Tami and Mr. Hawkins. Someone had said something crass in the locker room, and it was still rattling me. Mina saw something was up and thought some handball might be in order. The rhythm had a way of settling our middle school selves, and we kept at it as light faded. I smashed one and watched it sail past Mina as a piercing whistle silenced the yard. My rush of triumph deflated like a popped handball when I saw my dad at the side gate of the school, far away but close enough that I could read his body language. Shoulders rigid, chin jutted, his large frame aglow with irritation. He walked toward us with slow control, but I knew the coiled anger was there, waiting for fewer witnesses.

He stopped a court's distance away, his barrel chest puffed and commanding. I looked at Mina, who was watching my dad and me. She must have understood a lot about us in that moment, and she must have seen an opportunity, must have read my dad for the sport enthusiast he was, and managed to do what I was not capable of, what had not even occurred to me as a girl always trapped in cage of her father: Mina played into a fatherly pride that I hadn't known was there. She walked over to my dad as her tallest self and said, "Hi, Mr. Slater. My name's Mina, and your daughter is beating the socks off me in handball. I think you should know you've raised quite a player."

Without waiting for any acknowledgment, she made a left turn and calmly went to retrieve the ball, letting my dad and I have the moment. We watched her tall, strong body that could have belonged to a sophomore in high school cross the expanse of the school yard. I looked around and noticed that we were the only still figures on the blacktop, and that the dozen or so kids still playing had no clue about the wordless drama unfolding between my dad and me.

It put things into perspective. Suddenly, our private battles and secrets shrank as the solar system spun around us. There were countless other people with struggles and battles and secrets too, and yet they still were a part of this bigger thing, revealed by this public space where children spent their school days connecting across all the divisions our society kept inventing.

I could hear the satisfying steady rhythm of Mina's ka-thunk ka-thunk as she dribbled the ball on her way back to the court where my father and I were still statues. Her eyes were trained on the ball and the music she was making with its bounces. Then she looked up at my dad and said, "Wanna have a turn? Biff'll probably beat you too. But if she doesn't, I'll give it a shot."

"Biff?"

Mina offered no explanation, only a slight eyebrow lift.

And that was it. I watched as the boy in my father came out to play on the blacktop that afternoon, all long-legged speed and high yelps of glee at any fine strike — his or ours. With a keen sense that my dad was a competitive creature and a lover of all sports that require a ball, Mina gained entry into the heart of my father and made a place for herself in our home, such as it was.

That day I caught a glimpse of truth and reconciliation as circumscribed by ball and bounce, born between two people whom I loved despite, and because of, their imperfections. I saw a small seed of what is possible between us when the disconnect drops away and we can coexist in a sweet ka-thunking syncopation.

We were the last ones on the blacktop that day, slamming the ball in grand Vs over and over. A trajectory that, from a distance, would have looked like we were carving the curves of hearts with that liver-pink ball — half-buried hearts, only the twin arcs visible, but hearts nonetheless, rising from the goodness of our common ground.

HOLLYWOOD ENDINGS

FRANK CASTELLUCCIO

A version of this story was previously published in *RFD Magazine*.

The first night they met, Ikal walked Roy home and they kissed in the courtyard, enveloped by the scent of night-blooming jasmine, while the captivatingly warm Santa Ana winds danced furiously around them, sealing that first kiss with a magic neither had ever known. It was in the Hollywood Hills, in a bright pink 1940s apartment building reminiscent of a Mexican hacienda, that the two lovers first found happiness. The courtyard was an oasis filled with luscious palm trees, regal aloe plants, tall polished jades, glamourous ferns, and a majestic purple bougainvillea that had, long before Roy and Ikal were ever there, blanketed the walls of the two-story buildings to form what looked like a horseshoe. Along the borders, in the shaded areas, multicolored impatiens stood at attention waiting for their daily watering. Dozens of terracotta pots left by prior residents brimmed with cactus plants and unfulfilled dreams. This was the place where their love story began.

* * *

Ikal's journey to that moment started on a cool, dry morning at dawn in Santiago El Pinar. In his room, his record player spun as the needle skipped in a lazy rhythm on the final groove of the record that Ikal had listened to over and over the night before. "Yo No Naci Para Amar" was a melancholy tune about a young man who believed he was never meant to love anyone. He turned the player off, put the disc back in the sleeve, and stacked his records atop the cabinet, making sure they were completely aligned. His textbooks on drafting and architecture sat neatly on his desk, and his hand trembled as it passed over the covers in a goodbye caress. He clicked off the reading light, shouldered the bulging backpack, and took one last look out the window. Santiago El Pinar, a small town in the Chiapas region of Mexico, was his birthplace, a ghost town filled with living souls trying to escape.

His mother stood before the stove, a wooden spoon in hand. As he walked into the kitchen, the familiar morning scents greeted him: freshly ground coffee brewing, sweet anise rolls baking, and eggs sizzling in the large frying pan that never seemed to leave its place on the stove.

"Mijo, estas seguro? Tal vez tu padre pueda ayudarte," his mother said, wanting to know if he was sure, maybe his father could help. She tried to avoid his eyes as she wiped the kitchen table.

"Me tengo que ir," responded Ikal. "No puedo ser un narco. Me mataran si no hago lo que dicen." If he stayed, he'd be forced to work for the drug cartel. He had to leave to protect his family.

She finally looked him in the eyes. "No se por que pregunte. Se que estas haciendo lo correcto." She knew he was doing the right thing even before she had asked the question. She walked him to the door, took his arms, and turned him toward her. Looking deeply into his eyes, she made the sign of the cross on his chest to bless him and said, "Que Dios te cuide." Without another word, she opened the door, releasing him into the unknown of the deserts and the mountains that, until now, had always inscribed a limit for their family.

* * *

With every step he took, the unforgiving sun kept reminding Ikal that death could come at any moment, without mercy or reason.

He would never speak to anyone about the things he had done to gain favor to make the crossing, or the things that had been done to others, or of those that perished. Six days of walking, waiting; always hungry, always thirsty, and so tired … all snipped from the reel of memory, dropped to the cutting room floor.

* * *

The first thing he did when he arrived in the City of Angels was phone his family, to get word to them that all was fine. He was well, and he had arrived safely.

East L.A. was not what he expected. His cousin's building looked like a prison with all its windows dressed in security bars. He heard children shrieking through the walls and wondered if they ever played outside. The two-bedroom apartment was already crowded with his cousin's children and other members of his wife's family who had recently made the trip from Mexico. Ikal would have to sleep on the floor in the hallway on a twin mattress purchased from a secondhand shop.

On the day he arrived, he stood naked in the bathroom looking in the mirror affixed to the back of the door. He tentatively touched his left upper thigh and turned to look at the side of his body, which was tender and bruised from bouncing around inside the trunk on the way from San Diego with three other men. He sat on the edge of the bath and looked at the blisters on the bottom of his feet, strands of bloodied sock still stuck to his flesh. He lifted his hands to his face and looked at them closely. They were scratched and blistered from never releasing his grip on the backpack he had carried. He had done his best to clean up during the journey but, based on his cousin's wife's reaction, knew how he must have smelled.

"Mijo! Por favor! Ahi esta el baño, ve!" she had said, pointing to the bathroom.

He stood for a long time in the shower, watching the water turn brown as it poured down his body, spin around the rim of the drain, and then disappear. He looked at his hands again, placed both over his mouth, and let out a muffled scream.

*　*　*

Meanwhile, three thousand miles away, on the other side of the country, Roy was anxiously getting ready for his trip to Los Angeles. He forced the zippers closed on his two suitcases. He had packed, unpacked, and repacked at least a dozen times, unsure whether he was taking too much or too little. He looked at the patchwork of photos and posters of his favorite actors and movies plastered on all four walls of his bedroom and smiled. He had always been certain that in a past life he had lived in Los Angeles and been part of the Hollywood Dream Factory. He knew he wanted to be an actor and was assured of his readiness after years at the Actors Studio taking classes in voice, movement, and character development, searching for his inner truth, and honing his craft in community theater. It was time to make it in Hollywood!

Roy had been planning this trip all his life but always postponed it one more year on his mother's request not to leave her. Having just turned thirty, he couldn't wait any longer. He finally convinced his mother that it would only be for six months, and that he'd return. Initially she accepted that condition. "Okay, if you promise you will be back. Don't make me come and get you!" she'd warned.

"I promise, Ma, I will come back," he said as his mother stroked his hair away from his forehead and smiled.

"You've always reminded me of a young Tyrone Power with your hair slicked back."

Roy's sister may have been more supportive of his decision had it not left her alone to care for their mother. "But you *will* be back, right?" his sister asked in a panic.

"I have to go now, or I never will. I know that." He offered a half-hearted smile to reassure her, but he could see that she knew he would not return.

His mother stood at the front door, arms splayed, a human barrier. She begged and pleaded for him not to go. "I'll lose you forever! I won't be able to go on for another day!"

"Ma! Really? C'mon, you know you are everything to me, but I have to do this."

She moved away from the door crying, giving him just enough space to pass. He kissed her on the forehead and promised once again he'd be back.

His heart wrenched when he started the car and pulled out of the driveway, but at last he was driving down the street. He looked in the rearview mirror and saw his mother in the middle of the road bent over in tears. He slowed for a moment, placing his hand on the gear shift, but instead of turning back, he reached for the mirror, looked at his reflection, combed his hair back, and tilted the mirror down so he could no longer see her as he drove away.

He would later tell Ikal that his drive was like floating on a magic carpet. He barely rested, and his excitement grew with each state line he crossed. When he entered California from Nevada, he burst into song, belting out "California Here I Come." He sang it repeatedly until his voice sounded like mice squeaking. From US Highway 101, he took exit 9A — Cahuenga Boulevard — Hollywood Bowl. He stopped at the first telephone booth he could find and called his mother.

"Ma! I'm here! It's exactly what I have been imagining all these years. One day we will make the trip together. It's gonna be great! You'll see!" he said excitedly.

"That's nice. I'm happy for you, really," she said flatly. "I need my heart meds renewed. Can you call your sister and tell her? She doesn't know her ass from her elbow when it comes to taking care of me." And then she hung up.

✳ ✳ ✳

On that first night, Ikal and Roy shared all that is kept in the depths of one's soul, all the secrets that are never voiced to anyone else for fear of being judged. They seemed to grasp all that had appeared to them between wake and sleep, all that had waited, hidden just beyond the shroud.

The garden became their temple, and they both cherished it for what they experienced and what they shared. In that courtyard, they found their home. Together they'd take care of it.

✳ ✳ ✳

At first, they met every three or four days, and then every other day. Ikal would show up showered, his shirt ironed and smelling like patchouli, always sighing once the door was opened — as if reading his first line of a scene.

"I'm glad you are here. I didn't know if it was good for me to come over," Ikal said as he rubbed Roy's earlobe with his thumb and index finger.

"You say that every time. You know I'm waiting for you!" Roy said as he took Ikal's hand and kissed the palm of it.

Ikal sometimes stayed the night, but he always left before the sun came up.

Roy didn't know exactly where Ikal lived. He'd told him it was somewhere down La Brea Avenue but never gave him the address. "I'm beginning to think you have another man hidden somewhere. That's why you never give me your address. Are you cheating on me?" Roy asked, half kidding, half serious.

"I would never cheat on you!" Ikal said, his brow creased with consternation. "Ever! If either of us ever falls in love with someone else, it *must* be said. No cheating, ever!"

Roy looked at him, smiled, and caressed his face.

Their usual place, Hoy's Wok, was at Hollywood Boulevard and Cahuenga. It had four tables inside and two on the sidewalk. Roy called it a restaurant, but it was really a takeout joint. The windows needed to be cleaned, and the tables screamed out for tablecloths and flowers, but the place was sweet. For five dollars they'd get pork fried rice or lo mein, chicken with garlic sauce, or boneless spareribs, tiny things that Roy referred to as "pork chips." He would stare in amazement at the amount of hot sauce Ikal put on everything. "Doesn't that bother your stomach? Do you even taste the food?" Roy would always ask.

"Yes, I can taste it. I'm used to eating spicy. This is really not that hot," Ikal would respond, without looking up, as beads of sweat glittered on his face and forehead.

If they could scrape together forty dollars between them, they would head to Mickey's in West Hollywood, the bar where they had met. When the pair walked in, both men and women turned to look. Roy was fair-skinned, tall, and lean, with jet-black hair and deep green eyes. Roy's confident and elegant gait often made those who walked past him wonder whether they had just seen their favorite movie actor. Ikal was also tall, but his skin was silky caramel, and he took pride in his muscular frame, earned by the hard manual jobs he accepted (but needed to constantly change due to his undocumented status). When it was his turn to be carded at the door, Ikal nervously handed his fake I.D. to the bouncers, but they barely looked at it. "Welcome," they'd whisper while handing it back to him, gazing with bedroom eyes. "Go ahead — maybe a drink later?" His piercing black eyes and long black hair captivated everyone. The bartenders nicknamed him "Mayan Prince."

Getting there before 7:00 p.m. meant tap beer for a dollar, served in plastic cups. They drank several, and when late afternoon turned to evening, they would order Long Island Iced Tea. The combination of vodka, tequila, rum, and gin always did the trick. By this time, Roy headed for the dance floor, but it took Ikal at least another drink before he could get up the nerve to dance. He would stand on the side and smile as Roy jumped up and down, spinning and yelling, "I LOVE THIS SONG!" Roy would then drag Ikal onto the dance floor, where the two danced until their bodies were soaked with sweat. When Tammy Wynette and The KLF sang "Justified & Ancient," it signaled that the night was over and the bar was closing.

Once outside, their ears buzzed and the sounds of faraway muffled voices surrounded them as men and women left the club. Ikal would then take Roy's hand and insist they go to the beach. Roy would cite the late hour but relent when Ikal pleaded that they go look at the stars. Roy would smile and say, "Only because it's like a movie."

The next day, hungover and exhausted, they would always make the same agreement. "We cannot go out when we have to work the next day," Roy would scold. "From now on, we go out only on the weekends." Somehow, they were always able to find those forty dollars, and the following week it would inevitably happen again.

* * *

On those rare days when they had a day off together, Roy planned trips to his favorite Hollywood sites: cemeteries. There they would stroll past the graves of long-gone actors, Roy tutoring Ikal on their place in film history. "You see, the thirties and forties were the golden age of Hollywood. That's when stars were really stars. When they made the classics! It was glamorous. It's exciting! You can feel it, right? The magic?" Roy would say.

"Exciting? Doesn't that mean happy? Everyone is dead here. I don't know why we should be happy," Ikal responded.

"You don't get it. It's not about happiness. It's different for me. I grew up watching these people. It's like I know them personally." Roy would take Ikal by the hand and pull him about the cemetery. Then he would add how each legend had died. "Fatty Arbuckle, sad story, dead at forty-six of a heart attack — he never really made a comeback after being accused of rape. John Barrymore, he's over there, died of cirrhosis of the liver — great actor. Oh! And over there, that's Peg Entwistle ... poor thing jumped off the Hollywood sign … only twenty-four, couldn't make it once talkies came in. But she's a star now! Yup, those were the years when Hollywood was really Hollywood!"

Ikal smiled at Roy's excitement. "I don't really understand. It's all so sad, but if it makes you happy, then I'm happy for you."

*   *   *

Roy and Ikal celebrated their first Thanksgiving together. Roy's mother was not happy; it was their first time apart on a holiday. Ikal and Roy ate dry turkey sandwiches with lots of mayonnaise, drank ice-cold beer, ate pumpkin pie bought at the supermarket, and made love throughout the day. "I am very thankful that you're here with me," Roy whispered in Ikal's ear. "This is the first Thanksgiving that I'm not depressed."

"Maybe next year you can make a real dinner? I see on the commercials they have a lot more food on the table," Ikal teased while chewing on the last of his sandwich.

"Shut up! This is all we can do this year. It will be better next year, you'll see. I have a bunch of catering gigs lined up. We'll make this Christmas special."

*   *   *

Early December, on a ninety-degree day in Bel Air, Roy drove up a long curving driveway to a massive mansion sheathed with thousands of miniature white lights made redundant by the piercing sun. Fake snow had been strategically placed on the perfectly manicured grass, sprinkled around bushes, and piled on flowering plants so as to cover the blooms. Inside, the house was a Christmas wonderland; the air was scented with pine, and Bing Crosby crooned "White Christmas." On duty, Roy stood by a blazing fireplace in the middle of the living room holding a tray of hors d'oeuvres. Like the rest of the staff, he wore a red silk bow tie and a red velvet tuxedo jacket. Although the air conditioning blasted throughout the house, Roy sweated profusely. He caught a glimpse of two women in fur coats standing by the sixteen-foot Christmas tree as a photographer snapped their picture. Other guests, wearing wool sweaters, hats, and scarves, waited alongside for their photos to be taken. To no one in particular Roy suddenly blurted, "You people are nuts, batshit crazy! I'm going home for Christmas!"

He called his sister and asked if she would help with the airfare. "I'll pay you back in a couple of months. I promise."

"Like you were coming back in six months, right? Fine. It'll be a break from Mom," she replied.

He broke the news to Ikal delicately. "I'll be back in a week. I just have to go and see my mom for a few days, and then I will come back for New Year. We'll dance all night long!"

"Your family is important to you. It's good that you can go. I would too if I could." Ikal held his breath and pretended to wipe dust from his eyes.

The night before Roy left, they went out for drinks. Ikal hadn't eaten much that day and gulped three Long Island Iced Teas in quick succession. Nothing Roy did could get Ikal on the dance floor. Stone-faced, he sat watching Roy, until he rose and walked out of the bar, unnoticed.

Roy spotted his broad shoulders in the small park across the street, where Ikal sat alone on a bench.

"Please come back," Ikal said without looking at Roy. And then a sob erupted from his lungs, and he bawled so hard he couldn't catch his breath.

Roy sat and held him. "I could never leave you; of course I'm coming back. Where is this coming from?"

"I have no one that cares for me. Only you! Only you! You can't leave me! I can't go home anymore. *You* are my home." Ikal was slurring and clutching Roy like someone about to fall off a cliff.

"I'll always come home to you, always," Roy said as he wrapped his arms around Ikal. He rocked him back and forth until Ikal finally stopped crying. That was the last time Roy ever saw Ikal cry.

✳ ✳ ✳

The next day they drove to LAX. Neither mentioned the night before. As Roy's flight was called, he stood before the gate, looked at Ikal, and said, "I've been waiting all my life for you. Nothing is going to keep me from coming back."

Six days later, Roy walked up the ramp to the same spot and found Ikal in an ironed shirt, smelling of patchouli, and holding a bouquet of flowers from Ralph's grocery store.

"You're a nut!" Roy said as he hugged him.

Ikal rubbed Roy's earlobe, but they didn't kiss until they were in the car. "It's good you are back."

"It's good to be back. I couldn't wait to come home. It's time to take the next step."

✳ ✳ ✳

Roy spent days getting the apartment in shape so that Ikal would feel at home. He cleaned, made space in the closet, bought new towels and sheets, and even regrouted the bathtub. It was the first time in Roy's life that he would live with someone other than his family.

A car pulled up at the corner of Hillside and El Cerrito Place. A young man dressed in black jeans and a black shirt dropped boxes on the sidewalk, and joggers on their way to Runyon Canyon zigzagged around them. Roy still had no idea where Ikal had been living, or with whom. He wanted to make the stranger feel welcome, so he said, "Hi! I'm Roy!"

The man got back in the car, waved to Ikal, and said, "Orale wey." Then drove away.

"Who was that?" Roy asked. "Why didn't you introduce me? Why didn't he say hello?"

"Just a guy. He had to leave. It's not important," Ikal said as he started hauling things in.

"It's important to me. In my world, people introduce people to each other. Everything with you is so cloak-and-dagger. I feel like I don't exist sometimes, like you don't tell anyone who I am or what I mean to you."

"Why do we have to tell anyone? As long as we know who we are to each other and what we mean to one another, that's all that is important. It's no one's business."

Roy stood for a moment. He lifted a box, shook his head, and followed Ikal.

* * *

Their life became an unorganized routine. They worked when work was available. They went out to clubs and window-shopped at trendy boutiques on Melrose Avenue, never able to afford anything. They ate dollar Chinese food and celebrated birthdays with inexpensive gifts, always promising that next year would be better.

One late afternoon while sitting on the beach waiting for the blue sky to turn dark, Roy announced, "I'm going to stop thinking of this crazy idea of becoming an actor." He paused, waiting for Ikal to disagree with him, but when he said nothing, Roy continued. "I've fallen out of love with acting. I'm not even sure why I wanted to be an actor. I like the attention, but … perhaps if I had come here in my twenties." He looked at Ikal, expecting something.

"What do you want to do?" asked Ikal.

"I want to make money. I'm tired of just scraping by. I want to buy those things we see. I want to eat at a real restaurant. I want to be able to pay the electric bill!" They both laughed. Roy continued, "Maybe we can open a business together, right?"

"That would be nice," Ikal mumbled. "It's going to be hard with no money."

"That's what credit cards are for. And maybe you can start taking classes at night, study architecture," Roy mused. "You always say you want to be an architect."

"When I was a small boy, I always drew houses. I see how they look inside of them in my head. It would be like my dream come true if I could do that," Ikal responded in a lively, bright tone.

"We just have to figure out what we can do that's going to be successful," Roy said. "We'll make it work; you'll see. We've come this far together — we'll make it together. And once you get your green card, we're going to travel the world. It's going to be amazing! You'll see."

Neither looked into the other's eyes as Roy spoke those words. Instead, they looked at the ocean while Roy made small circles in the sand with his finger. Ikal reached out and took Roy's hand in his.

"Maybe," Ikal said softly.

* * *

Unhappiness took hold of them at some point, but neither could recall when. Roy hadn't been able to find a new career that inspired him. He still scraped by with catering jobs, organizing homes of the wealthy, and living the life of an unemployed actor who no longer had the dream of becoming a star. Ikal's frustrations grew with each job he had to leave whenever someone in human resources found out his documents were fake. Defeated, he would need to search for another unfulfilling job yet again. Their desperation boiled over, searching for someone to blame, and naturally they went after each other.

Both played a good game of chess. They instinctively understood which piece would be moved and precisely when it would take place, so neither could ever call checkmate.

"Have you decided about leaving?" Roy managed to say, attempting to hide his anger but failing miserably. He stood by the kitchen sink, having removed the Teflon from the frying pan he'd been scrubbing for an hour.

Ikal had spent the night out — again. Not with anyone special, Roy was sure of that. Still, it drove him mad not knowing and not having been warned in advance. He'd had another sleepless night wondering whether Ikal was safe.

"No, not yet," Ikal responded quietly. "I don't know if I should leave. Do you want me to go?"

Neither was ready to commit to leaving or to staying. Roy had always thought if Ikal could, somehow, become a legal resident that maybe, just maybe, his demons could be exorcised, and he wouldn't live in constant fear.

"Don't start that crap with me!" Roy exploded, slamming the now decimated frying pan against the sink. Roy found Ikal's indecision exasperating. They were stuck on a merry-go-round trying to jump off, but both too hesitant of taking that first step, afraid of falling.

"And now you start!" Ikal replied, crossing his arms.

"I won't make any more of your decisions! I've had it! You hear me?" Roy yelled. "This time I've had it!"

Roy manipulated Ikal's feelings by detailing all that he'd done for him, all he'd given him so he would stay. "I went into bankruptcy to pay for your attorneys. They all promised they would find a way to get you a green card. And when that didn't pan out, I borrowed money from my family to pay a woman to marry you. It wasn't my fault she changed her mind. And now you are ready to abandon me because you can't put up with me, because you find me difficult?"

"I'll never be what you want," Ikal said. "I never asked you to do anything for me."

"Sure, you never did. But you wanted a green card, you wanted to be legal. And I did it for you, and now this is how you repay me. Ready to walk out just when I need your help the most?"

"But do you take care of me because you love me," Ikal asked resentfully, "or because you pity me?"

It continued this way until the room got quiet. Roy walked outside and sat on the steps leading down to the garden. There he smoked a cigarette and cried silently, wiping away one tear after the next, annoyed at their wetness.

Then Ikal stepped outside and sat beside him. "We need to water the impatiens. It was very hot today." Ikal put his arm around Roy and rubbed his ear.

"Yeah, I know. They look like they are about to drop dead." Roy leaned his head on Ikal's chest. "It's getting more and more difficult taking care of everything …"

In solitude, Roy brooded on their five years together. It seemed like a lifetime. Five years of arguing, of loving, of making plans that never came to be, of making love, of throwing empty (and sometimes full) bottles of beer against walls. Five years of hoping that the other would change, of wishing that discussions of money, or lack thereof, were not always excuses to rip each other apart. He wished that the differences in their cultures were not justifications of their incompatibility. Whenever Ikal played Banda or Ranchera music, Roy would inevitably lower the sound saying that the "yelling" gave him a headache. And when Roy would make Ikal sit through one of the many romantic movies he watched, Ikal would comment on the unrealistic premises and eventually fall asleep. They simply never saw eye to eye.

But sometimes, when they fell into their four-poster bed and Ikal put his head near Roy's and rubbed his earlobe with his thumb and forefinger, they were both brought back to that place where they were alone, completely apart from the world, completely devoid of any problem or difference. How they clung to each other. Was it out of love or was it out of fear of being alone? Neither could make sense of it.

The magic of that first kiss on that first night so many nights ago became a legend. That moment could no longer sustain their existence together. Both were tired of hearing the other's explanations, excuses, or resolutions.

✳ ✳ ✳

As a couple, they emitted mixed social messages. Gregarious Roy had always welcomed strangers with open arms, but Ikal was cautious of people and kept mostly to himself. Ikal believed Roy was too quick to trust — that was how you ended up getting hurt. Roy blamed Ikal's standoffishness and mistrust of people as the reason they had no friends.

The only exception was Greg and Bert, an older couple who lived across the courtyard. Greg and Bert had been in Hollywood for many years, having run away from their strict Baptist families in Baton Rouge.

Greg and Roy often confided in and trusted each other, while Bert and Ikal, though cordial and friendly, kept their cards close to their chests, reserved and skeptical. According to Greg, he and Bert never *argued*, they *discussed*. "It's the Southern way," Greg proclaimed in his rich baritone drawl. "It's the only way." But when Greg got really angry at Bert, he'd declare, much in the same fashion as his favorite movie character, Scarlett O'Hara, that Bert was "as useless as a fly on an old man's dick!"

Greg's devotion to help the young couple get through their rough patches seemed sincere, but one day Ikal overheard Greg tell Bert that the only reason he and Roy were together was because they looked "marvelous together, just marvelous!" Then the mean-spirited Greg added, "It's dreadfully sad they haven't a thing in common!"

＊ ＊ ＊

Roy's stubbornness and histrionics made him unable to simply let go, while Ikal's marbleized emotions and predetermined devotion made him incapable of understanding the concept of breaking up.

"Why can't life be like a Hollywood ending?" Roy once asked Greg.

"Because Hollywood endings are only the beginning, my dear."

The couples often dined together. Roy liked setting a folding table and plastic chairs in the middle of the courtyard. He and Greg strung lights, draped the table with a silver foil tablecloth left over from one of Roy's catering jobs, and scattered petals from the flowers in the garden. Above them, to the right of the Hollywood sign, Yamashiro's restaurant stood on a hill, all lit up. As evening grew dark and the warm wind encircled them, Roy's perfect Hollywood magic moment was set. But as the night progressed, with too many cocktails and bottles of wine, conversations intensified and voices got louder. One misunderstood comment between Ikal and Roy resulted in a screaming match.

"Darlings! Dining with you is like stepping into one of those loathsome scenes between George and Martha in *Who's Afraid of Virginia Woolf?*" Greg stated grandly.

Bert looked over to Greg disapprovingly and said, "Now, Greg, let the boys be," as he sipped on his double bourbon mint julep.

Roy didn't appreciate the reference but understood it for what it was. Ikal didn't, and that made him more frustrated, insecure, and angry — emotions he took out on Roy.

* * *

One night, Greg and Bert returned from dinner, and as they walked through the courtyard, they heard Roy screaming.

"Dear God," Greg mumbled, "those boys are going to kill each other!"

"Let them be!" Bert said. "Live and let live, they'll figure it out." But instead of following Bert inside, Greg stood in the shadows and listened.

"How could you send them our rent money?" Roy yelled.

"I didn't send it all. I'm sorry — they really needed it," Ikal said.

Roy continued yelling, "Why do you always do these things without consulting me first? Why is it always behind my back?"

"I thought I could work extra shifts and have the money back."

"I can't take this anymore! All they do is take, take, take! Never once have they returned any of the money you lent them! Why doesn't your family cross over like everyone else and get jobs?" Roy suddenly stopped and looked at Ikal standing with his hands balled up in fists. Roy had never seen him so angry. They had a rule: Never to go after each other's families. Roy had broken that rule.

Roy took a step back as Ikal advanced on him. But instead of striking Roy, Ikal kicked one of the cats across the room. The cat jumped up looking astonished and crawled under the sofa. Then Ikal walked out.

Furious, Roy ran around the apartment opening cabinets, looking in closets and then under the kitchen sink. Behind the garbage pail, he found the toolbox. He opened it and reached for the hammer. He ran toward the front door but came to an abrupt stop, grabbing his chest. Roy fell to the floor, tried to catch his breath, and then curled into the fetal position.

Ikal didn't see Greg as he ran by him crying. Greg waited for Ikal to leave the courtyard before going into the apartment. When he saw Roy, he yelled, "Jesus! Are you all right? Ya'll are going to be the death of me!"

"I'm okay, I just need a moment." Slowly Roy stood up, looked around the room, and walked to the liquor cabinet. He grabbed a bottle of scotch and poured himself a shot as he had seen leading men in movies so often do moments before their inevitable doom.

"You cannot go on like this. It's madness, do you hear? Madness! No love is worth this much pain." Greg took

Roy's hand in his. "You've got to end it. I know the thought is devastating, but you've got to end it!" He paused. "Do you want me to stay?"

"No, I'll be fine," Roy said quietly as he took another shot of scotch. He looked up almost as if he were looking through the ceiling toward heaven. "I know what I need to do."

"All right, but I'm just across the way if you need me. Don't do anything foolish though, you hear?" With that Greg walked out, gently closing the door.

*　*　*

On a perfect sunny Sunday morning in Los Angeles, a slight breeze made the leaves on the palm trees dance a slow, sensuous dance. Ikal had come back sometime during the night and had fallen asleep on the couch. Crushed beer cans lay strewn around him like crumpled unfinished love letters. Roy had taken the two cats in the bedroom with him and had fallen asleep in the midst of purring and the haze of scotch.

Roy opened his eyes and looked up at the ceiling. He held his hand to his mouth, and as his body jerked forward, he leaned over the edge of the bed and heaved in a bucket. He hung there, motionless, hearing the familiar sounds of Ikal preparing the large pot of espresso that they always shared. As the smell of coffee reached Roy's bedroom, the doorbell rang. Roy lifted his head and looked toward the closed bedroom door. Ikal never answered the door when someone knocked, never answered the phone when it rang; he was always afraid of the unknown. Roy still didn't move. If no one answered the door, it would all simply go away. But the bell just kept ringing and ringing. Finally, Roy lurched to his feet and staggered out of the bedroom. Ikal, pouring milk and sugar into two cups, looked at Roy, perplexed.

Roy opened the door and laughed nervously when he saw the two men. They didn't look anything like they do in the movies. Instead of suits and ties, they wore jeans and T-shirts. Flashing a badge, one of them stated in a steely, diplomatic tone, "We're from the Immigration and Naturalization Office. We're looking for Ikal Costa Nunes. We understand he is living here."

Roy turned to find Ikal looking at him with terror in his eyes. Roy tried to speak, attempting to tell the agents that there was no Ikal here. "Perhaps next door? I was angry, you see …" He blushed, made frantic meaningless gestures with his hands. "The scotch. It was too much!" Then he screamed, "I made a terrible mistake!"

The cups crashing on the floor made Roy jump. Ikal ran to the back door. The agents barreled through the door and chased after him, ordering him to stop as they pulled out their guns.

Roy clutched his chest again, trying to catch his breath. "There's been a mistake!" he wailed. "Please, there's been a mistake!" But before he knew it, Ikal was handcuffed and being escorted out. Roy followed them outside to a waiting van.

In the courtyard, Ikal, no longer struggling, gazed at the wilted impatiens. He turned toward Roy, eyes fixed on his, and said, "Who has made the hideous, the hurting, the insulting mistake of loving me, and must be punished for it. George and Martha, sad, sad, sad."

The officers looked confused.

"Te quiero mucho mi amor," were the last words Roy heard Ikal say.

Roy stood in silence as the van pulled away. Alone, he touched his own earlobe, slowly caressing it as Ikal had so often done. He looked up at Greg and Bert's windows and noticed Bert peering down at him. The old man looked shaken as he reached to open the window. But then he stopped midway, shook his head, closed his eyes, and drew the curtains closed.

Roy looked around as if it were the first time he'd ever been there, like someone searching for something but having forgotten what. He looked up toward the Hollywood sign, tears streaming down his face. "Words …" he whispered to himself, "that's all they were supposed to be."

Roy entered the apartment. He was about to close the door but stopped and left it ajar. In the kitchen, the mugs lay shattered on the floor. He walked to the couch, stepping over the empty beer cans, and sat holding the pillow that Ikal had slept on. In time his eyes fell upon Ikal's backpack tucked under the coffee table. He felt his pulse throb in his ears. He opened the backpack and found old copies of Penny Savers, real estate brochures featuring homes in Beverly Hills, a catalogue from the Los Angeles City College, a worn Spanish/English paperback dictionary, a tattered, dog-eared copy of *Who's Afraid of Virginia Woolf?* and, folded inside, an expired one-way ticket to Guadalajara. Lastly, a Hallmark card, the envelope bearing his name in Ikal's handwriting.

He looked around the empty apartment, seeming to wait for the music to swell and the words THE END to appear. He opened the card.

WINDOW WALKING

RYANE NICOLE GRANADOS

Sometimes my sister, Prose, and I go window walking. Our walks are timed to follow a trip to ToGo's Pizza, because that's when Mercy starts her cleaning frenzy. She doesn't ask for help. She says we never get it just right, but she does decide there is to be no walking on the mopped floors, no stepping on the vacuum lines painting the carpet canvas, no sitting on the fluffed couch, and — most importantly — no breathing near the streak-free windows, mirrors, glassware, and Clorox-cleansed countertops. So, we walk. Around the block and around the block again because they haven't yet built a stoplight at the corner, and to cross the street in the dark would be a game of hit and miss, cars vs. pedestrians.

As we walk, the sun settles behind the 405 and the streetlamps buzz until they finally find the strength to burst into light. Then, as if an electrical circuit connects the Aves, porch lights, kitchen lights, living room televisions, headlights bound for home, and city lights begin to shine brilliantly throughout the streets. Prose has decided that the evening's sudden illuminations are a daily Fourth of July.

You can see so much more when you walk the streets than in the portrait revealed from a car's passenger window. You can see the goings on of families sitting down to dinner, friends swapping saucy secrets, marriages breaking up, husbands returning home, baby's first steps, boy's first kiss, girl's first taste of the reality that her father's not invincible and her mother doesn't have all the answers. When window walking, the soul of the world appears between the drawn curtains of Los Angeles.

Miss Maige lives in the window three Ave apartments away. On the first floor, behind an old oak door, within the pale-yellow walls seen through the four-foot glass pane is Miss Maige, quilting a lineage of kinfolk into an oversized linen. It's a family quilt to be passed down from Ave to Ave, or a covering for visiting grandchildren, and even a drape protecting the house from the quick-witted wind outsmarting the loose brick designed to plug the apartment hole.

Roxanne lives in the window above Miss Maige. Only seventeen but on her own because there's no longer room for her in the foster home. The suits lowered her rent and send her checks every month and come by to make sure she goes to school and has no one else living there. Roxanne will be eighteen in a few months, and Roxanne will have to find a business suit of her own.

Roxanne has a lover that she kisses at night. He's nineteen and in the Marine Corps. When he visits, he scares off the stoop squatters who wait for her to walk home from school. They don't whistle anymore, but they still watch. They watch the straps of her backpack trace the side of her breasts and they long to be the weighty books that bounce off the back of her acid-wash jeans.

While Roxanne's lover fights to defend her magnificence, she enjoys the hungry stoop squatters' stares. She rolls her hips and bites her bottom lip, giving them the thrill of a lifetime as if a supermodel on her own personal runway. When she reaches her step, she makes sure to look back. She makes sure that they're positioned before she blows their minds. Softly, as if kissing satin, Roxanne presses the palm of her hand against her full lips and gives wings to a flirtatious kiss. Her admirers lean over the railing of the stoop as if catching a ball hit into the stands at Dodger Stadium. They cheer, slap high fives, and then quickly turn to make sure Roxanne's lover isn't patrolling the Aves.

He knows nothing of her daily ritual. When he calls upon her, he finds her waiting in the window. Waiting and reading. The books once housed in her bouncing bag now lie sprawled out on the living room floor. For Roxanne, these books hold the secrets to life. Roxanne reads and waits for her lover's return. She reads out loud to herself so that the breath of each story can dance a waltz in her ears. She reads until she hears the starched stiffness of his uniform ascending the stairs.

"Hey bookworm, tell me a story," he says. And she does. Roxanne recounts tales of Tish and Fonny on Beale Street and Romeo and Juliet in Italy. From beginning to end he listens and then rewards her with a kiss. He kisses her in the dimly lit corners of the room and of her body. Their shadows melt together, creating a silhouette of tenderness for all who walk by to see.

Sometimes when Prose and I window walk, Roxanne peeks over her shoulder, similar to the way she glances at the stoop squatters, and winks at us. She winks while we watch until her lover's hand fumbles for the curtain's edge, sliding it closed and capturing their love inside.

In the window across from kissing Roxanne live Marcus, Ketura, and their six-month-old daughter, Babygirl. When she was born, they had yet to decide on a name, but when Mercy stopped by with the crib that James and I had slept in and Prose played in (because she liked the way the night sky colored the spaces between the crib bars more than she enjoyed sleeping), Mercy gave Babygirl the name of a queen. Born on the day of Sauda's passing, Babygirl's given name is Danielle Sauda Hall. Sauda because it's only fitting for a baby that looks doused in dark chocolate; Sauda because it creates a legacy of strength and power to be reborn in the future of the Aves; Sauda because, "It was simply the right thing to do," explained Mercy. And Danielle after Daniel because everyone needs a good Christian name. Like my name, Zora, Sauda is the type of name a baby has to grow into. Until then, for her sake, I'll call her Babygirl.

In the window below Babygirl's crib, you'll find the Viramontes women untangling their tresses. Angela, pronounced *Anhella*, is in my grade and has been in my P.E. class for the last three years. Every day, no matter what the occasion, she wears her hair in one long braid that she winds and winds and winds again into a neat bun above the nape of her neck, risen like a freshly baked donut almost too perfect to eat. I hate the bun she wears to camouflage the curls.

Our window walking has exposed a wave of thick black hair long enough to sit on and strong enough to swing from. If I owned her windstorm of hair, I would spin in circles, letting its length cloak me like a superhero's cape. I would frustrate my enemies by flinging my hair on their desk during journal-writing time. I would run my hand from scalp to hair's end and twirl sections around my index finger to get the attention of the cute older boys. I would brush it with one hundred strokes a day to keep its shine like the fashion magazines suggest. I would wash it with strawberry shampoo and let the suds sink in until the entire bathroom smelled like the strawberry patches of Orange County. I would do so much if I had Angela's hair, but I would never, no matter what my sisters or mother did, or brothers expected, or father demanded, wrap it away from the eyes of the world.

Every apartment has four windows that face the sidewalks paved up and down the Aves. Each window is a camera lens revealing a picture of the Aves' soul. As Prose and I window walk, we're photographers taking mental photos of untold splendor. But Prose, cupping her hand into circles around her eyes, prefers to think of us as top-secret agents peeking through binoculars at unsuspecting targets.

When the sun finally reaches the base of the 405, only moonlight guides our path between the too-far-apart streetlights with flickering bulbs struggling to stay alive. And when the cars have found their way home or the porch lights have witnessed the last key in the lock, it means it is time to end our window-walking tour. We can smell the aroma of the Aves. Orange and blue gas flames on stoves work hard to give sustenance to the starving belly of the Aves. The stoves' heat and the frying pans' grease are suffocating, and windows fly open, freeing the smoke and smells of the culinary creations.

Prose grabs my hand. She's old enough to be an undercover agent and curious enough to watch Roxanne's lover cup her entire breast like a baseball, yet she's scared of the night sounds and shadowy images that accompany our return home. The humming in the streetlamps seems louder, the arguments in the apartments are clearer, and the figures at the bus stop or the next block are threatening until we get close enough to see familiar faces. I would never admit this to Prose, but I need to hold her hand too.

When we get home, Mercy is waiting on the porch. After every house cleaning and every window walking, she waits for us. With our fingers behind our back, we count down her litany of criticisms and remarks. One,

"Where have you been?" Two, "You better not have tried to cross that street at night." Three, "You know it makes me uncomfortable when you stay out this late." Four, "You're not little boys you know, you're girls — you do know this, right?" Five, "I don't know where I got you two from." Six, "Dinner's ready, hurry inside." And as we run up the stairs, we stop at the door to allow Mercy her final statement: seven, "Girrrrllllls, take those scruffy shoes off and don't mess up the lines on the carpet." We giggle but never loud enough for her to hear as we acrobatically tiptoe around the carpet's edge.

DRIFT, LONGSHORE

KARTER MYCROFT

The weekend was done, and the garbage on the beach had to go somewhere, so before the sun rose he put on his big orange raincoat and went with his trash bags and long plastic claw to the edge of the strand. Great waves crashed and sizzled over the breakwaters, provoked by high winds that whipped his cheeks as he started his task. A rare summer storm here in South Bay.

He worked his way from the first rocky groin to the next, clawing up all manner of refuse. Beer cans and lime rinds. Plastic snack trays picked clean by the day shift of seagulls. Abandoned sunscreen. Spent vape pens. A waterlogged cellphone the sea had stolen and spat back up, as if unsure how to use it. He fished a decent pair of sandals out of the shallows and put them into a secondary bag to evaluate later. One man's trash, and so on.

It was hard work in the wind and the rain, with only a dismal predawn glow for light and an extreme glut of garbage strewn everywhere. But it didn't make him angry. He didn't fume and curse to himself about how inconsiderate the beachgoers were, not like he used to. Every Monday morning since the boat burned up he'd come here to clean up after the weekend and he believed it was the first good thing he'd done with his life, so he was resolved not to complain. On some level he even enjoyed it. It was good to be the only person out here, scouring the sand with the dark waves to one side, the microjungle of ice plants to the other, alone with his claw and his trash bags. By the time the sun oozed through the townhomes up the cuesta he had cleared the first strand and was crossing over the second rock wall to the next.

When he first saw the woman, he thought she must be dead. She and her beach chair were soaked with rain, caked in wet sand, and utterly still. He dropped his bag and rushed to her side.

"Good morning," she said. He'd never seen anyone else on the beach this early, and certainly not in this kind of weather.

"Are you okay?" he asked. His voice came out rough and he cleared his throat, still crouching beside her beach chair. He realized he must have looked terrible, with his scraggly beard and long wet hair, his grimy orange raincoat and double layers of clothes beneath.

"The tide will be in soon." Her voice was flat and emotionless, and she spoke so quietly it was hard to hear over the hiss of the waves. "You can't clean the whole beach."

He stood, considering this stranger and what she'd said. She must have been freezing cold, but she lay in her swimsuit and straw hat like the sun was ablaze in the sky. She was pretty, he thought, in the same way a fish on the deck of a boat is pretty: mostly because she was not where she should be. Her eyes drifted coldly from his face to his trash bag, almost like she was accusing him of something.

"Well, someone has to clean it." He sounded more defensive than he'd meant to. The woman only shrugged, so he went on past her to claw at bottles of rain mixed with beer dregs, a waterlogged roll of toilet paper, the tatters of a ruined blue tarp.

Morning came muted through the clouds. The rain let up some, and the sun cast a rust-red glow across the sand. He clawed and bagged the garbage with a greater fervor than before, as if the woman's comment had been a challenge. As if he somehow needed to prove he'd earned the right to do good deeds. He thought of his boat, the way the flames raged above the harbor, the looks in the eyes of his crew when he told them he'd never have work for them again. Why shouldn't he be the one to tend to the beach? He had nothing but time on his hands, now.

The shock he felt upon crossing the third groin froze him still in his tracks on the rocks. Up ahead someone was walking in the surf. It was the woman in the straw hat, and she was approaching him. Moments ago, she'd been behind him. He wondered if he was going crazy.

"How did you get here?" he asked once she was in earshot, his voice tense with anxiety.

"The trash is like the tide," she said, as if that explained everything. Rainwater drooled off her hat and pattered near his feet. "It will just come back."

He stood up straight and narrowed his eyes. He'd always assumed, if he did run into someone, they'd be thankful for his efforts, or at least leave him to his work. But this woman seemed determined to discourage him. He felt indignant. Taunted. She eyed him with a look of casual disgust, like he was the worst piece of trash on the whole beach. It reminded him of his mother, the way she'd stood for hours on the dock, staring blankly at the empty berth where their ship had once moored.

"You're right," he said. "I can't clean everything. But I can clean this" — (jabbing his claw into a swim cap) — "and this" — (snatching a filthy sock and shoving it in his bag). And he stepped around the woman and went on.

He saw her a third time as he returned. By now the rain had cleared and the tide was in, and he trudged through the surf with four full bags of garbage, the most he'd ever collected. She was swimming in a tangle of kelp, letting the still-heavy waves crash over her, pasting black hair across her face. Her eyes followed him as he walked, wide and glaring, full of salt and judgment. He thought of lobbing a bottle at her head just to make those eyes close. She made him feel guilty. She made him feel like the man who'd burned down his family's ship for insurance money, not the man who spent half his mornings cleaning the beach. Was it impossible for a bad person to do good? What did goodness or guilt mean to the ocean anyway?

She said something, her voice lost in the crash of the waves. "I don't care," he responded without knowing what she'd said. He felt exhausted now, his shoulders aching. The surge pushed the woman back, and he watched her disappear into seafoam. That was the last he saw of her.

"I don't care," he said again, to himself. He continued up the beach.

By the time he reached the parking lot, the last of the rain had stopped. The sun was bright as yellow flames on the concrete, and he could smell the tang of drying rain in the ocean air. He loaded the trash bags in his truck and tossed his claw on the passenger seat as he sat down.

Halfway home the urge to stop came over him, and he drove to a lookout he knew up in Palos Verdes, where the land curled back on itself and a grassy knoll overlooked the sea. He parked and sat for a time with his hands on the steering wheel. Sunseekers filed onto the beach, carrying blankets and bottles and picnic baskets and everything else that people without ships took to the sea. He watched them come and go and scanned the waves for signs of a black-haired woman strewn with kelp. All he saw were surfers, parents with their children, and the static of distant garbage on the sand. Later, he drove to the dumpster, threw out his trash bags and went home, leaving his coat and his claw in the truck until next time.

LOOKING FOR JOEY

TISHA MARIE REICHLE-AGUILERA

Eva Dominguez sat in her car Tuesday after work in the parking lot at Norman Houston Park, waiting for her counselor friends to join her for their weekly hike. She texted her sister, Catarina: **Any news from Joey?**

Their brother had been MIA for ten days. At his sixteenth birthday dinner, he'd announced that he'd be going to homecoming with a boy. According to Catarina, their very Catholic parents had exploded and Joey had run out with his backpack. Eva cursed herself for the umpteenth time. Why hadn't she been there to intervene? Instead of taking the fastest route — 405 to Manchester — she'd taken surface streets from her apartment in Palms to her parents' home on 89th and Ruthelen. She'd cruised east on Venice Boulevard slowly, turned along National through the area that had been developed when the Expo Line was built. Her parents' businesses flourished after the train line was fully operational, enough so that they bought a modest home in South L.A. that was now worth about double the purchase price. A home that wasn't Eva's at all.

Cat replied: **Nada. He shoulda known better.**

Eva gritted her teeth. For a moment, she doubted Cat was concerned about their brother at all. Her spoiled ass always took their parents' side. Eva responded: **Known better than to be his real, true self?** Eva fumed as she dictated the message: **Maybe your parents should be angry at themselves for not supporting the son they claim to love!**

Their reaction to Joey's news reminded Eva why she avoided them. At thirty-five, she didn't need to be scolded about her lapsed faith or criticized for not being a wife and mother. That night she had delayed her arrival by meandering through Los Angeles streets without thinking until she made a left onto Manchester, then she'd deliberately passed Van Ness so she could drive by the park on Saint Andrews Place. Joey'd loved going there as a toddler. Back then, she'd spent every Saturday that she wasn't working with him and Cat. They had so many adventures: parks, museums, the beach, once even an overnight to the San Diego Zoo. But when Mamá found out they'd slept in on Sunday, too tired for mass, "Ya no!" she'd proclaimed. Since then, Eva and Joey had not been especially close. He was, after all, almost twenty years younger, but he knew she led a support group for LGBTQ students at Dorsey High. He could've asked her for help. Her text to Joey on the night he'd left had been unread until midweek. He'd finally replied: **Fine. Staying w/friend.** When she'd responded, asked about school and if he needed any clothes, she'd heard nothing.

Eva looked at her other texts. Her friends were still about fifteen minutes away. Usually when Eva arrived before everyone else, she'd park up the hill at Anita's and they'd walk down together. But Anita had back-to-school night, so she wouldn't join them until after the hike, for dinner.

Anita and Eva had been friends since they were both at Linwood Howe. Eva had stopped a fifth grader from bullying fourth grade Anita, even though Eva was only in third grade at the time. Anita had gone to LMU, finished her degree and credential in four years. Her house on Don Zarembo was a graduation gift from her parents and grandparents. Well, at least the down payment was. When Eva finished Cal State Dominguez Hills, the only thing her parents gave her was a gold crucifix blessed by the pope that she promptly donated to the silent auction at Saint Augustine where Cat was in school. If Mamá recognized the donation, she never said anything.

Cat replied: **They love us as long as we do what we're told. You know that.**

Eva couldn't respond.

Cat added: **Or as long as they think we are. I told J to play dutiful son another year and a half. Be freely gay in college.**

Eva: **You wanted him to live a lie?**

Cat: **We all do.**

Eva stared at the three teenage girls playing soccer in the grass and pretended her sister's words didn't hit that painful spot in her memories. She was too restless to wait in the car, so she got out for a few warm-up laps around the park. She jogged slowly, took long strides and deep breaths. As she rounded the third corner, on the far side of the park, she saw a pair of fairly new retro Jordans sticking out of the bushes at the end of two jean-covered legs. She slowed to a walk. They looked like the shoes she'd bought Joey for Christmas last year. He'd wanted the brightly colored J Balvin ones, but those were way out of her budget. She approached, cleared her throat. "Hey there. You okay?"

The legs didn't react.

Eva stepped off the track, looked back toward her car. Only a few others remained in the lot. Eva walked closer, gently tapped one of the exposed shoes with her own. "Excuse me, sir?"

No reaction.

She used the volume usually reserved for a room full of teenagers. "Sir! Are you okay?"

Still no response.

Eva pulled the bush back a little and peered at the body. Not Joey but about the same age, probably still in high school or just out. His shirt was ripped; there was dried blood and fresh bruises on his face. "Shit!" Eva knelt, checked his wrist for a pulse. Faint. She patted her pocket, but she'd left her phone in the car. "Son-of-a—" She whistled at the soccer girls and called out, "Call 911, tell them we need an ambulance."

The oldest one responded immediately. She repeated exactly what Eva'd told her to the dispatcher then ran toward Eva and put the phone on speaker.

Eva yelled, "Young adult male. Weak pulse. Evidence of facial injury." She lifted his shirt to look for other injuries.

He moaned.

"Semi-conscious. Maybe abdominal injuries too." Eva put her palm on the young man's forehead, lowered her volume. "Help is coming. Can you tell me your name? Who did this?"

He moaned again, tried to mutter something.

Eva put her ear closer to his head. "Tu nombre? Que pasó?"

He gurgled, "Jo … Man …" and something that sounded like "dirty" or "thirty." His lips kept moving but no sound came out.

Distant sirens wailed until they were so close that Eva's ears buzzed.

Through blurred vision, she watched the EMTs work on the body, relieved that those shoes were not on her brother's feet. She covered her face with her palms smelled the boy's sweat and the faint odor of Axe body spray. She gasped. He could be somebody else's little brother. "Is he gonna be okay?"

The EMT shrugged. "We don't know the extent of his injuries. They'll check at the ER."

"Which hospital?"

"Centinela. You can follow us."

Eva walked behind the EMTs slowly, as if with weighted feet. They rushed not-Joey across the grass to the waiting ambulance. She heard a familiar voice call her name repeatedly. Then two soft arms wrapped her up and held her until her shaking subsided.

Grace offered Eva an unopened bottle of water. "There's a policeman who needs to talk to you." She pointed. "Can you answer a few questions?"

Of course there'd be police. Her favorite park was now a crime scene. Eva squinted at the figure, backlit by the setting sun. As she got closer to the man in uniform, the familiar face opened into a broad grin. For just a second. Then he stood straighter and scowled, like he was mad at himself for breaking character, for letting himself remember he had once loved Eva.

✳ ✳ ✳

Anita's tiny frame filled the patio outside Fiesta Martin as if she was six foot six, instead of only four-ten. "Why the hell didn't any of you call me?" The couples at the nearby high-top tables cringed, but Eva didn't flinch. She was the one who had taught Anita how to stand taller, puff up, and project her voice. So, Eva took a long drink of her margarita and smiled out one side of her mouth before answering. "You were working. That's why I texted."

"Where were you two?" Anita poked Daniel's arm and lifted her chin in Grace's direction.

Grace poured Anita a glass from the off-menu pitcher, a perk of knowing the family that owned the restaurant. She and Anita had gone to LMU together, and she now worked at a rival high school closer to the beach. "I got delayed in the world's longest IEP and didn't get to the park until almost dark." She raised her eyebrows up and down suggestively.

"And I," Daniel hung his head in shame, "was at the wrong park." He was the youngest member of their counselor cohort, having started at Hamilton High the year before last. He'd had it rough in high school, barely graduated because he'd been bullied so much and had no support at home. After years of working in the corporate world, he felt it in his heart that helping other gay high school boys through the struggle was the right career choice. "When I realized my geographical error, Miss Thang here was too busy playing first responder to answer my texts."

"More like playing detective," Grace teased.

Anita sat next to Eva and elbowed her. "What are these chismosos implying?"

Eva rolled her glass of now only ice between her palms, like she rolled her pens when they were running out of ink. The coolness soothed her but the rattling clearly annoyed Anita.

She grabbed the glass out of Eva's hands. "Wanna tell me why you aren't talking?"

Eva took her glass back and stretched it out to Grace for a refill. "Thomas."

"Thomas?" A long pause. "Oh, Thomas." Anita put one hand on her friend's arm.

Grace handed Eva her an almost overflowing glass.

She sipped. "He was ... *is* the investigating officer."

"The what now?" Anita narrowed her eyes.

"He's gonna call later. Take my statement." Eva took a much longer sip.

Anita turned sideways on the chair and softened her voice. "You talked to him already?"

"A little. It was fine. We were — cordial." Eva looked away. "He looked happy to see me at first, then must've remembered." She took another drink, moved an ice cube around inside her mouth. She had broken up with Thomas after an exam revealed she couldn't have kids. The only thing he had talked about more than becoming a police officer was becoming a dad.

Anita picked up the glass that Grace had poured for her and downed it in one gulp.

Eva whispered, "Am I terrible that I'm just so glad that half-dead kid in the park wasn't Joey?" She shared the similar shoes and the physical damage to the boy's body, the way he'd moaned, barely conscious.

"No!" Anita snapped. "I'm glad he wasn't Joey, too." She half-hugged Eva.

"She was about to follow the ambulance straight to the hospital," Grace said. "But I told her she couldn't go on an empty stomach."

Daniel leaned against Eva. "You know how *hangry* you get."

"They're right." Anita dipped a chip in salsa. "I'll go with you after we eat."

"That kid's parents must be so worried." But Eva wasn't sure her parents would be if she had found Joey all beat up like that. She sought comfort in chips and guacamole.

Anita looked around and said, "I have a good distraction for you all." And she proceeded to regale them with the antics of the Culver girls who had painted themselves all blue — her school's colors — and streaked across the football field while the parents were being bored by the principal's welcome speech. "They had on swimsuits and swim caps, but they ran so fast that everyone thought they were naked."

Daniel raised an eyebrow. "They didn't know the principal was gonna be boring. Why'd they *really* do it?"

She grinned and opened her Instagram, read aloud: "'Blue Streak: rapid changes required in girls' sports.' They were protesting the unequal distribution of practice field time. Football monopolizes sixth period and after school, even in the off season."

"Some activists you've got there." Grace patted Anita's arm. "Wish my students would be that passionate about something. Anything!"

"Can I see that?" Eva took Anita's phone without waiting for a response. "You can look at what your students post on Instagram?"

"Of course." Anita took her phone back, clicked on something. "If I follow them. And I follow most of the student groups."

"So they can see what you post too?"

"Only on my public profile: MIZA2Z. See?" She handed her phone back to Eva.

Daniel showed her his CounselManDan posts. "But they can't see my private pics."

"Those are mostly shirtless selfies?" Grace asked.

Daniel feigned embarrassment. "Only the ones at the gym."

"Grace, you do this too?" Eva asked.

"Not a private one. My arms are too short for selfies. I only post school-related stuff for the college center: SamoCollegeBound."

Eva searched for Joey's name and variations of it on Anita's Instagram. "Jo-Man-thirteen," she whispered. "That's what the kid at the park was trying to say. Maybe those *were* Joey's Jordans. Maybe the kid in the park was with Joey before he was attacked." She shoved another chip in her mouth and stood up so fast she knocked over her chair. "Take my tacos to the hospital. Please." She guzzled the rest of her water and practically jumped over the patrons at nearby tables in her rush to leave.

"Hey!" Anita yelled. "My phone!"

"Go with her!" Daniel said. "We'll make your chimichanga to go too."

Anita grabbed her purse and sprinted after her friend.

✳ ✳ ✳

When they got to Centinela Hospital, Eva shoved past people and demanded to see the injured boy.

"I'm sorry," the nurse said, "but if you aren't family —"

Eva smacked her hand on the counter. "I found the boy at the park. I think he knows something about my missing brother."

"Security?" the nurse yelled.

Instead of the graying guard getting off his stool, Thomas stepped out of the hallway and into the waiting area where Eva and Anita stood.

"Da-yum," Anita muttered in Eva's ear. "He glowed up!"

Eva swatted her away. But she wasn't wrong.

"I was about to call you, Eva. I wanted to check on the kid first." He reached into his pocket. "This yours?" He held out an evidence bag containing a gold, diamond-encrusted, cursive-D charm hanging on a gold chain. "The clasp's broken."

Eva stared at the jewelry in Thomas's hand and reached for the pendant around her own neck — a capital D, no bling. She sank into the nearby wall.

Anita held her up before Thomas could offer his help. "It's Joey's," she said. "Hi Thomas."

He scribbled on a notepad. "Anita." He nodded at her, more serious than he'd been at the park.

Eva knew Thomas had blamed Anita for their break-up, but she'd never told Anita that, never told Thomas what had really made her end things with him that summer after they'd graduated.

"Where'd you find it?" Eva asked, afraid of the answer.

"In the vic — the kid's hand."

Eva tried to picture the boy's other arm but could only recall his damaged face. "Did he say how he got it? How he got the shoes?"

Thomas scowled. "He hasn't said anything yet. When I got here, he was sedated. But he's stable. I should get to talk to him in about an hour." He stepped closer to Eva. "Are you're being honest with me about everything that happened? Did you see anything else?"

Anita let Eva stand on her own. "It's gonna be a long night. I'll get us all some coffee. You two …" She walked away shaking her head.

Thomas guided Eva away from the other waiting families to a pair of corner chairs. "What aren't you telling me, Eva?" His voice had softened a little with Anita gone.

Eva took out her phone. On the drive over, Anita had downloaded Instagram and set up a basic profile for her: MIZD2. Anita was her only follower. She had one post with the Dorsey High logo. She searched for JOMAN13's public posts and showed Thomas a group selfie at Loyola High's football game. It was a little blurry. "I think that one in the back is the kid from the park. He must go to Joey's school."

"Who is Joey?"

Eva blinked hard. She hadn't talked to Thomas in so long. He didn't even know she had a much younger brother. Clearly he had not kept tabs on her the way she had on him all these years. She knew he had been married but wasn't anymore — not sure why. He had no kids as far as she could tell. She knew he'd gone to the LAPD academy after two years at West L.A. College. She even knew his younger sister was a district administrator in the South Bay. But he clearly didn't care what had happened to her. "Joey is my little brother."

Thomas exhaled hard. "I thought you were gonna say 'son.'"

Eva scowled. "And you worried he'd be yours?"

He looked down at the bag in his hand. "More like I hoped," he said quietly then shook his head hard. "Not possible." He fake-smiled. "So, you have a brother in high school?"

Eva nodded.

"I bet that made Catarina happy. To have a someone around after —" Thomas cleared his throat. "She in college now?"

"Mount Saint Mary's."

"Wow. Private schools. Your folks must be —"

"My parents are the reason Joey is missing. And my sister doesn't seem to care."

Thomas grimaced.

Eva explained the birthday dinner argument and how she blamed herself for not being there. "And I think the boy in there knows where Joey might be." Eva inhaled deeply.

Thomas put a hand on her shoulder and whispered, "Why didn't you ever call me?"

Eva exhaled hard and stared into his eyes. "Can we focus on finding Joey, not on us?"

Thomas stood up so Anita could sit next to Eva and got all business-like again. "Right now, my focus is on that kid in there." He looked at the Instagram post again. "You got a name?"

Anita took the phone and tapped the screen. "Write these down." She spelled out the five Instagram handles tagged in the photo. "They're all private accounts, but maybe your IT can get their real names."

"And find Joey." Eva stood up and grabbed Thomas's arm. "If I help you get the boy's name, will you help me find Joey?" Thomas took her hand off his arm then moved away. "I can't make any promises." He walked back down the hall to wait until he could talk to the boy from the park.

✳ ✳ ✳

When Grace and Daniel arrived with food, Eva was on her third cup of coffee. And she didn't normally drink coffee. She paced the waiting area and couldn't sit down. She looked at photos on the Loyola High website. She sent a screen shot of the IG post to her sister.

Cat responded instantly: **Bald one is Max something. On baseball team with J.** And she agreed to message him so Eva would stop bugging her.

"One down, four to go."

They waited a few more hours, but Thomas never came out of the room.

Eva went home and waited up all night for his call that never came.

✳ ✳ ✳

The next morning, Eva left Thomas a message, called in sick to work, and drove to Loyola High. She argued with the principal's assistant, insisted she had an appointment to speak with Dr. Frederick that she didn't really have.

He couldn't tell Eva anything because she wasn't on Joey's emergency card.

Eva showed him the Instagram post and asked if he knew the other boys.

He couldn't reveal names but agreed to give Eva's card to the ones he could identify in the photo. "But I don't know that one." He pointed to the boy from the park.

Eva deflated.

"I hope you find Joey. We miss him around here."

Instead of going home, Eva went to Anita's, sat on her back patio searching social media obsessively. She messaged random student groups at Loyola asking if they could relay a message to Joey. She texted Cat again for an update.

Anita got home from work early, worried about her friend. "You could have gone inside," she said, handing Eva a grease-spotted bag from Popeyes. "Figured this might cheer you up." She plopped down on the matching chaise lounge.

"I don't understand why Joey didn't feel like he could confide in me." She turned to Anita, eyes damp. "If something terrible has happened to him, I'll never forgive myself." She shoved some fries in her mouth.

"You offered your place. That's all we can do for kids. Let them know we are here when and if they need us." She slurped her soda. "They're at that age where they think they know everything, think they can fend for themselves."

"Damn underdeveloped prefrontal cortex!" Eva smacked her own forehead with her palm, winced at the pain she inflicted upon herself.

"You wanna drive around some of the night hangouts Daniel mentioned and see if we can find some boys?"

Eva looked over at her, almost grinned.

"I heard it. But you know what I mean." Anita reached over for one fry. "Let me change and I'll drive. Maybe we walk around. We don't find anyone, at least we got some exercise."

As they cruised along Hollywood Boulevard, Eva stretched her torso out the window, squinted into the dusk. It wasn't until they were headed back toward La Brea that Eva had some hope. "Slow down. I see some kids." There was a group perched on the picnic tables and leaning against cars outside In-N-Out.

Anita put her hazards on and waited for a few cars to go by before she backed into a metered space.

Eva jumped out of the car, ran past the group, and grabbed a young man by his shoulder.

He spun toward her, fists clenched at his side. "Bitch! I wish you would!" His face was fuller than Joey's, and he had a jagged scar along his hairline, an injury that should've been stitched up but clearly had not been.

Two of his friends flanked Eva, and she raised her hands in surrender. "Lo siento." She covered her eyes. "I know better. I'm so sorry. I'm just —" She took a deep breath and tried to channel her counselor self, but her mama-bear instincts were still raging inside. "I thought you were my brother. He has been missing more than a week, and I wasn't thinking rationally."

Anita added, "We were hoping to find him or some of his friends hanging out here."

Eva's phone lit up with a notification. Cat replied: **Maybe he doesn't wanna be found.**

"Damn her!" She told the three boys about the birthday blowout. "And I feel like it's my job to keep him safe now. Since my parents won't."

"If my dad was calling me names like that, I'd've left too," the tall friend said.

He and the other friend relaxed a bit, but the young Latino she'd been so sure was Joey smirked. "Your brother look as good as I do?" he asked.

"He has the same lineup in the back. Or he did last time I saw him." She could not recall when that was. "But it's probably grown out by now."

Embarrassed, Eva looked down and noticed the scarred boy was wearing the brightly colored J Balvin Jordans that Joey had wanted.

"You got a picture?" colorful shoes asked.

Eva showed them the Instagram post. "He's a junior at Loyola High. Plays baseball."

"He looks almost as good as me." Colorful shoes looked up at Eva. "I can see why you were confused. But I've never seen him. I'd remember."

"Maybe you know some of their social media names? Or whatever." She tapped the screen. "Where do you all go to school?"

Colorful shoes glanced at his friends with raised eyebrows. Instead of answering, he held up the phone so one could take a picture of the screen. "Tell you what, MIZD2," he put his hand on Eva's shoulder, "we'll show the picture to some people who might know Loyola people." He overenunciated the school name like it left a bad taste in his mouth. "And if we find him —"

"You'll call me right away?" Eva took a business card out of her phone case.

"No," he stepped back, "we'll tell him you're looking for him so he can call you."

The taller friend said, "If he wants."

The other friend added, "Sometimes, we don't want."

Eva felt the blood drain out of her limbs, pissed that Cat might be right. But what if Joey was hurt somewhere like his friend? She couldn't give up until she knew he was safe.

Colorful shoes reached out and squeezed Eva's shoulder gently. "Entendies?"

Eva nodded and leaned into Anita's nearby arms. She watched the trio walk away, barely felt Anita guide her back into the car. She didn't want to go home. She felt Joey could be nearby.

Anita turned on the car and buckled her seatbelt but didn't start driving. "Eva, I know you want to keep looking. But what if, like they said, Joey doesn't want to be found?"

Eva crumpled against the cool window, too tired to accept that possibility.

*　*　*

The melatonin Anita gave Eva helped her sleep for a few hours, but she still couldn't go to work the next day. She answered a few urgent student and parent emails from home before she called Thomas again to tell him she had some information and to insist they meet. She also texted Cat, asking if she knew any other places where Joey might be.

Cat replied: **Nowhere your barrio kids would be.**

Eva looked around for something to punch.

Cat added: **Private school kids are different. Look at Grove, Bev Center, or 3rd St Promenade.**

Eva couldn't even respond.

Thomas agreed to meet at the hospital where they learned the unknown boy in the Instagram photo was Joey's boyfriend, Gabriel. He went to Venice High. Said he was the one who insisted Joey come out to his parents. He didn't want them to be a secret anymore. He was wearing Joey's necklace and they had traded shoes. "My J Balvin ones were too colorful for me. But Joey loved them. I thought my family was cool with us, but when me and Joey held hands and walked down the street, mi tío attacked us. Joey was wearing my crucifix. That made mi tío madder. He yelled something about Jesus and jewelry. I'm pretty sure he was drunk." Gabriel sobbed, choked.

Eva gave him some water.

"My dad tried to stop mi tío, I think. It happened so fast. I told the cop all this already." Gabriel swallowed hard. "Joey ran toward the bus and that was the last time I saw him."

Eva took Gabriel's hand in both of hers. "Have your parents come here at all?"

Gabriel shook his head. "They won't. Not now. When I ran after Joey, they told me not to come back. That's how —" He closed his eyes. "It's all my fault," he whispered.

Thomas stepped in from the doorway. "I called a social worker friend who specializes in cases like this. She's gonna help Gabriel emancipate."

Eva wondered what a "case like this" meant, then looked down at the boy her brother loved. "You can stay with me once you're released."

"You don't have to do that." Gabriel looked up at Thomas. "Just find Joey."

The nurse came in to change Gabriel's IV.

Eva stepped away and looked at Thomas too. "We'll do everything we can."

Thomas motioned for Eva to follow him out of the room. "Just heard they found another young Latino who fits Joey's description. He's at Kaiser West L.A."

"Then let's go."

He put his hand up to stop her. "This kid is in really bad shape. Worse than Gabriel."

Eva felt her knees give out. Thomas put an arm around her waist and lifted her. "He's still unconscious, but the doctors are hopeful."

Eva steadied herself.

Thomas released his hold. "I'm not supposed to say that. But if it was my brother, I'd want to know."

For a moment, she wanted to feel Thomas's firm arm again, to feel that kind of comfort. She closed her eyes and imagined their life together with Joey as their kid. A happy, loved kid.

"You wanna ride with me or meet me there?"

Eva shook her head and returned to reality. "With you. But first," she went back inside the room. "Gabriel, I'll be back in a few hours with some clean clothes." Eva choked on her words a little. She took out business cards. Gave one to him, one to the nurse. "Call me if you need anything else."

Gabriel squeezed Eva's hand then closed his eyes before his tears could fall.

✳ ✳ ✳

At Kaiser, the nurse on duty told Thomas that they still had not identified the boy. He told the nurse that Eva might be the kid's sister, that she was helping him with an ongoing investigation.

The first thing Eva saw was the jagged scar along his hairline. "Oh, sweet boy." She sobbed and held his not IV'd hand. The machine's beeping rate increased. Eva squeezed his hand tighter, brushed her fingertips across his cheek. "Who did this to you?" She turned to Thomas. "Not Joey." She explained her own mistake at In-N-Out the night before. "He and his friends had agreed to look for Joey, to help me find the boys in that photo. What if that's what got him like this?" She sat in the nearby chair, covered her face with her hands.

"And you don't know his name?"

Eva sat up and shook her head. "But his friends! I have to find them. They could be injured somewhere too."

"Let me send someone."

"They'll never trust police. At least they've seen me and Anita before." She texted Anita who said when she finished her last appointment, she would pick up Daniel and go to In-N-Out.

"We tried to question the uncle."

Eva looked confused for a minute.

"Gabriel's uncle. The guy who assaulted him and Joey."

"You think he did this too?"

"You thought he was Joey from behind. The shoes. Uncle may have thought the same."

"You said 'tried to question the uncle'?"

"His wife is a lawyer. Told him he didn't have to say anything."

"Seriously?" Eva stood up. "Why would you cover for a man who —" She stopped, knowing full well what women do for men they love. Or ones they fear.

"And we don't have enough to arrest him. But I've got a photo line up to show this kid if — I mean *when* he wakes up. Right now, that uncle is our only suspect."

Eva paced the room with the rhythm of the machines. "Where is this kid's stuff?" She looked around the room frantically. "Maybe we can find his friends through social media."

Thomas took her arm and turned her to face him. "IT has his phone."

"They don't know what to look for." She wrenched herself out of his grip, showed him Joey's Instagram post again. "That bald guy is Max something. He plays baseball with Joey. Maybe he knows where my brother might be."

Thomas went out to the hall to make a call.

Eva returned to the boy's bedside. She took his hand again. The machine's beeping pace increased again. "I know you can hear me. Remember me from last night? I'm gonna do everything I can to find who did this. I promise."

Thomas cleared his throat. "There are two kids in the waiting area. Said they are looking for MIZD2. That you?" He barely held back his grin.

Eva wiped her eyes. It took a few seconds for the name to register. "Yes. Me." She shoved past Thomas and sprinted down the hall.

"There she is," the tall one said, almost happy to see her.

"You're a mess," the other one offered.

Eva blinked at her disheveled reflection in the glass and tried to smooth her hair back.

The tall one steered her away from herself. "Your man friend is fine."

The other friend said, "Too old for me, but you could do worse."

Eva blushed. "Did he show you the photos?"

"What photos?" the tall one asked.

"Of us?" The other friend looked a little worried.

"Suspect photos. Did you see who did this to your friend?"

"We saw him," the tall one said. "Tried to stop his drunk ass."

"I got video." The other friend took out his phone.

"You have to show Thomas."

"Your guy? Why?"

"What's he gonna do?"

Eva gulped. "He's a cop. But I've known him a long time. You can trust him." She bit her bottom lip, not sure how true that statement was. "He's the one helping me look for Joey."

"Your brother? Oh, we found him."

"What? You found him? Where?"

The tall one sucked in his lips. The other one gestured to zip his lips closed and locked them.

Eva sat. "I understand. But can you tell me if he's okay? His boyfriend was pretty badly beaten and said Joey ran away but —"

"Eva!" Thomas interrupted her rambling. "You can't tell everyone everything or else —"

"These are the friends. Show them the lineup." She turned to the boys. "Show him the video." She walked away to text Anita her location.

Anita responded immediately: **Great! Coming to you.**

Eva texted Cat: **Found J's bf Gabriel. Ask Max if he knows G's uncle.** Eva knew it wasn't likely, but wouldn't Joey's teammates be concerned? Want to help too?

Eva walked back to Thomas and the boys, felt like maybe the earlier tension had dissipated.

One of the boys put a hand on her shoulder and said quietly near her ear. "I messaged your brother. Told him we were here with Officer Delish."

Eva blushed. "How will he see your message if he doesn't have a phone anymore?"

"He's got one. Don't worry."

Thomas said, "I'm going to take them back to see their friend. Will you be okay here?"

Eva nodded, sat in a chair, and went back on Instagram to check for any messages.

Cat replied: **Uncle? You looking for a date?** Followed by the laughing emoji.

Eva didn't know why she even bothered with her sister. She really wasn't taking any of this seriously. Eva called

Centinela Hospital to check on Gabriel. The nurse said he was sleeping. Good. That gave her time. She went into the Target app and put socks, underwear, some plain black T-shirts, and comfy pants in her cart. "What else do boys need?" she muttered.

"Toothbrush, soap, deodorant, lotion." Thomas sat beside her and smiled. "If anyone asks, we got an anonymous video of the attack. These boys won't be implicated."

Eva smiled back. Added some Dial, Old Spice, and Suave with aloe vera to her cart.

"He'll also need some new shoes, but don't get those at Target." Thomas made a yuck face. "I have a few extra pairs that'll fit him."

"Gabriel?"

"Yes. And this kid." He exhaled hard. "They still aren't ready to give their real names. But he doesn't have parents who give a damn either." He pounded his fist into the arm of the chair. "I don't understand how anyone —"

Eva put her hand on top of his not clenched one. "Not everyone is like us."

Thomas unclenched his other hand and turned to face her. "Us?"

Eva looked away. "I just meant —"

"You gonna offer all three of them to stay at your place too?" he asked.

Eva snorted, turned back to him. "My one-bedroom apartment? Guess I could put bunk beds in the room, and I could sleep on the couch." She shook her head. "I have to do something."

"*We* can do something." He held both of her shoulders. "I have a place with plenty of space and if you want —"

Their moment was interrupted by Anita and Daniel bursting into the waiting area. She had a variety of Jarritos in a clear plastic bag. He carried two brown bags, and the aroma of Pinches Tacos filled the air around them.

Eva felt light-headed, realized she had not eaten all day.

"I know you!" Daniel said. "Always hungry. We brought enough for everyone."

Thomas patted her hand. "I'll go get the boys."

Daniel watched him walk away.

Anita raised her eyebrows.

Eva shrugged, took a long sip from the Tamarindo that Anita had opened for her.

She reached for her food, but Daniel held it up too high. "First, dish. And quick."

"Those boys found Joey. Told him I was looking. Said he has a new phone." She looked at Anita. "Why hasn't he called me? I want to help him."

Anita sighed hard. "You know why."

Daniel gave Eva her food. "Give him more time." To Anita: "That's not the chisme I wanted." He tilted his head toward Thomas and the boys approaching from the hall.

Eva stood up, a forkful of asada fries already devoured. She swallowed, sipped from her bottle. "How's your friend?"

Thomas answered for them. "Still unconscious. But stable."

Eva gestured for the boys to sit. "You remember Anita from In-N-Out? This is our friend Daniel. He's a counselor at Hamilton."

"My cousin went there! You know Latanya Roberts?"

They started chattering about other students, and Eva stepped back against the wall.

Anita offered Thomas a taco. "We've got al pastor, asada, pescado, and a few veggie." She unwrapped her torta. "Mine's camarón!" She smiled and took a huge bite.

Thomas looked at Eva as she was about to take another forkful. "That's not a taco."

"Asada fries. Fully loaded." She put it all in her mouth and extended the plate to him.

He hesitated. "I *am* starving. But good news first." He leaned in close to her, said quietly in her ear, "Officers arrested the uncle. He was drunk, ranted about how he tried to show those boys what a real man was and some other nonsense about sin and hell."

"Anything about Joey?"

Thomas rubbed her hand. "No. But if he says anything, they'll let me know."

She leaned into him as he ate a few bites of her dinner. Then Eva's phone rang. "It's an unknown number." She never answered those.

The taller friend looked up at her. "You need a new ringtone." He smiled.

Eva pressed the screen, put it on speaker. "Hello?"

"Heard you were eating my favorite fries without me."

"Joey?"

"I'm on my way, hermana."

EPIC STICK

THEA PUESCHEL

Dom kickflipped his skateboard in front of Mrs. H's mobile home. His long gray bowl cut bounced in his eyes; he tossed his bangs and shifted his weight on the board, maneuvering around a fallen palm frond, a likely victim of the Santa Ana winds.

"You're too old for that," Mrs. H screamed from her trailer's porch. She was dressed in a pink sateen nightgown. Her white hair was held in a perfect bun. The peaks of her cheekbones revealed she had been a beauty in her day.

A redheaded young woman in dark blue scrubs exited the trailer with a child on her hip and edged past the elderly woman. The toddler, dressed in firefighter pajamas, twirled his mother's hair in one hand and opened and closed his other in a greeting, but his attempt to get Mrs. H's attention failed.

Dom smiled and tick-tacked his board sideways in the middle of the street, inching closer to his mother's neighbor, and winked at her.

Mrs. H's cheeks flushed. "Don't get fresh with me, young man."

"Bye, Granny," said the redhead, laughing as she walked down the steps to the sidewalk and shooting Dom a conspiratorial wink. The toddler clapped.

Mrs. H glowered at Dom, then shifted her focus to her granddaughter and sweetly said, "I love you, dear."

Dom stumbled on his board and wondered how she could be so ill tempered with him, yet so generous with her granddaughter.

"La lu, gan nee," the toddler said, opening and closing his hands with ferocity.

Mrs. H smiled at the child and waved, then shot an icy glare toward Dom and slammed the door behind her.

Somehow, at fifty-five, Dom could tap into his ornery teenage-skateboarder self. It felt good to feel young, to feel as if he could still shred. He had completely forgotten what it was like. Now he was wreaking havoc on the mobile home retirement village next to the municipal golf course, just as he had terrorized the curbs and walls in front of his childhood neighbors' Granada Hills 1960s tract homes.

* * *

Dom had found his 1970s SIMS Pure Juice Kicktail Skateboard in the vinyl shed out back of his mother's trailer. The board's dull red wheels screeched at him from an open cardboard box, a welcome distraction from palliative care. When he ran his finger over its wooden edge, it awakened memories of ripping along Venice Boardwalk, carved forward with a rasp and clickety-clack of nostalgia.

"I won't die until that shed is cleared out," was the only thing his mother had said to him upon his arrival at her bedside, amid coughs and gurgles. She hated inconveniencing everyone but him. Her impending death left him with the responsibility of clearing out her home and the shed before her mourners appeared. Her hair and makeup were perfect and camera-ready as she reclined on the gray silk sheets of her bed. She had always been a planner, and leaving a beautiful corpse was a top priority.

Finding his first taste of mobility and freedom in a box had been a surprise as he dug through the paraphernalia of her acting career. He had assumed the board, like her cultural relevance, was long lost in the annals of time.

* * *

"It's almost time," Dr. Li said softly through the phone. "A lot of family members want to be there, for the end."

His mother had said she was dying for the first forty years of his life. The past fifteen years, however, she had accepted her longevity and told him she had written him out of the will and would probably outlive him, anyway.

Dom had cut his business trip short and hopped onto the plane from New York to Los Angeles while he daydreamed about a Hallmark movie reunion. He planned to sit next to her deathbed and tell her all the things he had spent an entire lifetime withholding. Maybe, just maybe, she would do the same.

Dom leaned against a white column at the airport and practiced his words under his breath as he waited for the LAX FlyAway Bus. It arrived with a squeal of brakes. The bus pulled away from the terminal and onto the road. As it merged onto the 405 North, he fantasized about holding her hand as she eased into the light or if he was going to be honest as she was sucked into the fiery pits below.

But when he arrived at her bedside, she was more alive than he had expected. The sweet moment he had dreamed of seemed far out, and increasingly improbable.

* * *

Dom skated past beige golf carts on their way to the municipal course. He paused in the middle of the street and did a 360. Proud that he nailed it, he skated on.

A teenage girl with long, blue-streaked black hair skated up next to him dressed in chinos, a Givenchy shirt, and checkered Vans. "Epic stick," she said with a smile. He gave her *the* nod.

"I'm Lupé. Never saw someone so old stick a 360 before."

He grimaced. "I'm not *so old*."

"Nice board." Lupé laughed and skated off, not looking back.

Growing up, girls had always looked back. But, then, he was something to look back to. Now he was middle-aged and delaminated, his thrasher youth and six-pack abs were a faint memory, even though he was still thin. His stomach skin had started to sag, and his happy trail had begun to depopulate and gray. No longer a cool skater boy that girls flocked to flirt with at the Galleria or Boardwalk, he was an old dude skating through a trailer park of ancient retirees. Yet Dom felt the need to showcase his virility. He was still young enough to father a child if he wanted to.

The staircase down to the community room offered him the opportunity to attempt a double set. Sure, he knew it would be burly and slightly dangerous, but he wasn't *that* old.

The staircase had four stairs, a platform, and four more stairs. He took a deep breath, calculated the perfect angle, and backed up. The board creaked. He pushed his right foot against the ground, left foot firm on the board, and skated forward as the wheels released a hollow scraping sound.

Dom caught air between the first set and the landing, and his board slammed the aged aluminum handrail, slightly coping. The wheel caught, and he wriggled it free. The board became airborne again and slid out from under his feet. He flew, or rather fell, from four or five feet. His board twirled as he barreled over it. He landed with a thud on his knees first, hands second, and chin third. A shock blasted through his body. Prone, Dom couldn't move for a few moments. He rolled over on his back and tried to steal air back into his lungs. Broken. He had fallen like this countless times four decades ago, back when he could pop up and dust off the knees of his Dickies, but getting back up wasn't easy now. Maybe he *was* that old.

He groaned and saw ravens fly overhead. He wiped his lip, and blood smeared across his face. His scraped hands had pieces of pavement and pebbles lodged in them. His tan slacks had huge holes in the knees and exposed his bloodied, scraped flesh.

Lupé skated up to him. "You okay, sir?"

Dom wasn't sure what hurt more, his body or being called "sir" by a fellow skater after an epic fail. He attempted to smile. Everything hurt, but most notably his mortality.

"You want me to call 911?"

Dom rolled the back of his head against the cement. "It's not an emergency."

"No offense, sir, but it looks like one." She winced. "You can't just lie there."

Dom writhed and throbbed with pain. An emergency room would take too long. He couldn't chance being away for several hours from his mother's bedside. He was waiting for the "I love you," and he wanted his Hallmark moment, dammit now that the shed was clean. The three words he had hungered for since childhood.

Lupé adjusted her beanie. "I'll see if my Grandpa Ollie can take you to the hospital. He lives here."

Dom groaned and gave in. "Yeah, that'd be good. Urgent Care will do."

She skated off and, in a few moments, returned with her Grandpa Ollie at the top of the stairs. When Ollie exited the orange pickup truck, Dom couldn't help but notice he wasn't that much older than him and in much better shape, with bulging muscles. Ollie's shirt slightly lifted on his way down the stairs, revealing a sexagenarian six-pack covered with gray fur. The shame and humiliation in Dom's solar plexus bubbled and stabbed.

"Had a bit of a spill, I see," Ollie said, sticking his hand out to Dom, who was still supine on the ground. "Let me help you."

"Thanks." Dom took Ollie's hand and sat up. The embedded gravel stung. Ollie levered him all the way to his feet. Dom couldn't help but feel his own weakness. "You're strong."

"I lift. It's just something to do," Ollie said with a smile, and a pec pop. "Let's get you to a doctor. Lupé, get his other arm." She put her arm through Dom's.

He didn't want to, but he hobbled arm in arm with Ollie on one side and Lupé on the other, carrying his board under her arm. The sensation of the circumference of Ollie's bicep in the crook of his arm busted what remained of his dignity. Mentally, spiritually, and physically, Dom was a poser. They walked up the wheelchair ramp that ran alongside the formidable stairs. Lupé slid across the truck seat to the middle and fastened her seatbelt. With a jerky motion, Dom sat beside her. Ollie closed the passenger door for him.

∗ ∗ ∗

Ollie's truck brakes juddered in front of Dom's mother's trailer. The smack of flesh on pavement left Dom sore from his toes to his ego. Nothing broken, only bruised. He shut the truck door and inched his way up his mother's driveway.

The screen door to the trailer opened, and the hospice nurse in rainbow scrubs stood there solemnly holding it open.

"Don't forget your board," Lupé said, rolling down the window and reaching behind the seat to hand it to him.

"You can have it," he said over his shoulder without looking back.

He walked past the nurse into the rhythmic sound of the wet, crackling respiration of near death. The volume of his mother's breath altered with each of his steps down the hall. By the time he stood in the doorway to her room, she took a deep breath and held it.

Dom's heart constricted as he urged his sore body forward to her bedside. Her exhale had yet to arrive. He reached for her hand, and his road rash brushed the silkiness of her sheets. Pain pulsed through him like hot shards of glass. Her hand, cool to his own, slid away from him.

"Not yet," said the hospice nurse from the opposite side of his mother's bed.

His dry lips cracked apart to make room for the words that pooled on the floor of his mouth and sat behind his teeth. "I —"

The exhale made its way free and escaped from his mother. It was long and labored and ended with a rattled hiss. He knew, and his eyes stung worse than his ego from the fall.

* * *

After placing his earbuds into his ears, he boarded the Amtrak Pacific Surfliner in San Luis Obispo. He chose a seat next to the window on the lower level of the train car, readying himself to be a passive observer of nature and topography. He turned up the volume on the Hawk vs. Wolf Podcast to quiet his inner critic (his mother's voice). Why had he shred? Hubris. Why did he leave in the middle of planning services? A grief counselor's suggestion. Why was he going to return? To officiate the memorial.

Looking at his hands, he saw the dull pink scars of the healed road rash on his palms; the stiffness remained. Dom squirted moisturizer into his hand and rubbed his palms together to soothe the dryness. His hands felt different. Two weeks had passed. He felt different. His sense of urgency was gone, but the dread of his mother's expectations in death remained.

Families, mid-chatter, boarded and climbed the stairs to the second level. Children intertwined fingers with their parents. The sense memory of his mother moving her hand away from him prior to her last breath kickflipped from his heart to his head. The pressure in his tear ducts increased. Dom looked away and steadied his eyes on the window and the parallel train tracks. Across the aisle, a frail older gentleman shouted into his phone the train's arrival time, competing with the podcast and Hawk's description of his latest fail.

The engine jolted forward, and the chimes of the train horn struck a chord and announced their departure. Another 360 or rather a 1080 for Dom, returning home but never quite nailing the trick of validation. Maybe it would be different this time, a permanent goodbye.

The Central Coast Pacific Ocean view of blue-to-dirty-green seawater and white sands blurred into the Santa Monica mountains of brown and yellow chaparral, through the sprawl of the squat industrial buildings and post-war tract homes of the San Fernando Valley.

"Next stop, Los Angeles Union Station," a voice announced.

ALL THAT CAN WAIT

NORIKO NAKADA

I usually don't notice, and even if I do, I try to ignore it. It's a low hum. Sometimes it's a rhythm, sustained for a second or two. It sits beneath all the other noises: the taps, the voices, the papers shuffling.

It comes from someone's backpack or pocket, and if I hear it, they hear it. Embarrassed, the guilty student usually quickly and silently fishes into the private depths of their jacket or bag to turn it off. There will be an apologetic look sometimes, but not always, and it really doesn't bother me. The buzzing, I mean.

What is more off-putting is the chirp, the electrical sequence of notes, or a snippet of a pop song ringing into our classroom. Those disruptions cause everything to stop as the guilty student offers instant apologies and turns all sorts of red. They understand that their electric disturbance has shattered our thoughts, brought our learning to a halt, and they feel bad, or they pretend to.

When it's just a rhythmic buzz, a hum, a vibration? I don't worry about it.

I heard it as I walked past the closet where I store my bag for the school day. Sometimes I leave my phone in there all day. It's my attempt to untether myself from modern technology. There is no reason for me to check in on social media, to get constant news updates, or post about what I ate for lunch. And friends and family know

I'm busy at work all day, so I know they won't bother to call or text.

There was, though, the familiar low buzz while I was in the middle of a lesson on one of my favorite poems. I didn't want to leave that headspace of "two roads diverged in a yellow wood," and "knowing how way leads onto way," I let the buzzing fade into the noise of the room. I know things can wait. Even if there is news on that phone that will change my life completely, that change can wait until after third period, or fourth, or until the end of the school day.

He was the one who taught me things could wait, mostly because he never wanted to wait for anything. Before I met him, I didn't believe in love at first sight or fate, but then, on the night we met at a West L.A. dive bar (the way people met before the internet), all of that changed. I sometimes wondered how my life would be different if I hadn't gone out that night, or if he hadn't. What if he'd lost my number or never called?

He was the one who made me get a cell phone in the first place, who insisted I always be within reach, and it was then, after we were comfortably in love and engaged, that he showed up unannounced at my classroom.

I hadn't checked my phone all day, and was teaching a different poem, Emily Dickinson's "I heard a Fly buzz — when I died," but I hadn't heard my phone. He had been calling all morning, though, and when he stood there, in the doorway, I could read the weight of bad news on his face. His father had passed, and his being there captured the tragedy of it all.

It was then that I learned news can always wait. Even if I didn't check my phone, life and death would go on. He always wanted me to be there to pick up. He wanted me to be a different kind of person. Maybe my inability to be there, no matter what, along with all the ways in which I made him wait, were the reasons he was gone.

So, when I heard the buzzing from the closet, I already knew life could change in an instant. We are reminded of this every so often when a slate-gray sports car changes lanes right in front of us and we swerve, avoiding catastrophe. Or we see the accident across the freeway median and catch a glimpse of someone on the side of the road who is no longer headed toward their destination. Maybe it's a news story about a hate crime, an untreated illness, a miscarriage of justice. I avoid watching the news because I hate staring at tragedy. Natural disasters, mass shootings, police profiling, refugees in crisis. How we find out about these moments, though, depends. These pivotal moments, the ones that divide before and after, we remember them.

I heard a Fly buzz – when I died – / The Stillness in the Room.

I ignored the buzz, waited in the stillness, pretended it wasn't there. After all, the students were bent over their papers, catching up on notes about the rhyme scheme, repetition, and the image of these paths parting in the yellow wood. I chose not to go to the closet to see about that buzzing. Maybe I knew something was wrong and was just delaying the knowledge. I returned to teaching, and it wasn't until lunch that I reached into my bag.

For an instant, I regretted not checking sooner. Daycare rarely called, and when I glanced at the screen and saw "Garcia Family Daycare," I wondered if Ava was okay. My mind raced through all the horrors of what could have happened. I closed my eyes, took a deep breath, and let my heart pound for another moment before reading through the messages. I had waited, but just like any other news, it hadn't mattered. Had I known several hours earlier or now, that wouldn't have made a difference, and it wouldn't have made this news any easier to bear.

I herded my students out of the room and closed the door. Then I started reading. I would need to take the rest of the day off. I needed to pick Ava up as soon as I had a chance. I called for coverage of my afternoon classes, wrote a quick lesson plan, grabbed my things, and walked to my car.

* * *

Whenever I drive through Los Angeles in the middle of the day, I wonder what all these people do all day. The streets are crowded, the restaurants bustling, and for a moment, I imagine what he might be doing. If he was around, would he be the one racing to pick up our daughter? I ignored this thought and rolled up on a red light. Doing this on my own was hard. It was nothing I would have chosen, but imagining an alternate universe with him in it never helped.

As I threaded through traffic on a bright, fall afternoon, I thought about calling Mom. That's what I usually did when I went to pick up Ava after work, but I doubted she'd be home. I tried her anyway, but she didn't answer. I checked the clock, 1:10. Mom was probably out to lunch with Dad or a friend. My sister would be volunteering at her kids' school.

I could call Angela. She was one of the other moms with her kids at the Garcia's. I wondered if she or her husband would be picking up their kids. What was she going to do? And then I thought of Naia, the mom with the new baby there. What were we all going to do?

I pulled up to the cute bungalow in Santa Monica splashed in robin egg blue paint. Murals of kids playing surrounded the outdoor play area where I often found Ava on the swings. It was quiet, as it usually was at pickup. I was always in awe of how they kept all those little ones content all day long when I could barely make it through a few hours. I wondered if today had been any different.

Mercedes was sitting at the table outside when I opened the gate. "Hey," she said, but she didn't get up, and I could tell, as hard as my day might have been, hers had been much worse. "Sorry to pull you away from work."

"No big deal," I answered, although I could imagine the chaos my fifth and sixth periods could make for a sub.

"Ava's sleeping. Do you want me to get her up?"

I wasn't in a rush. "No, I have time," I said as I pulled up a chair. "What's going on?"

Mercedes shook her head. "I don't know. They came and …" Her voice trailed off. "I guess I didn't have the papers in order for all of the girls." I could hear someone washing dishes inside. I looked toward the window. "That's my cousin. She's cleaning up after lunch."

I nodded. I didn't see anyone else. At pickup, the two sisters were usually outside playing with the kids, and Mercedes' cousin was inside with the babies. Now, I realized, the sisters were gone.

I looked for Esme and Erika. Mercedes shook her head. "They threatened to shut me down if they were still here." She wouldn't look me in the eye.

My heart ached for the younger sister, Esme. She had held Ava every day when I first started back to work. Ava loved her so much, and she was the one I was sometimes jealous of because, some days, when I came to pick my baby up, she didn't want to let go. Sometimes Ava would tug on her long, black hair, or snuggle against her small chest. Esme would always smile at me, though, a small, gentle grin, as she passed Ava on to me, as if to say, "She's yours again. Keep her safe until tomorrow."

Ava had been there for almost two years. This was the daycare he and I had picked out together. Mercedes had known he'd left when she saw me that Monday morning. He had always been in charge of drop-off, and there I was. I could read the questions in her eyes.

By then, Ava wasn't clinging to me at drop-off. She'd see Esme inside the toddler room and race over. That was just after she'd started walking. Ava was sleeping through the night, had adjusted well to daycare, and it was as if he'd been waiting for things to feel easier so he would feel okay about leaving. When he told me he was done, I hadn't seen it coming. I chose not to see it coming. I had been pouring all my love into Ava. Motherhood had changed me, had shifted something in my heart. It wasn't as if things had been all that great before; I knew about his indiscretions. I knew there was a gap in our relationship that hadn't been there before, but I figured things would work out.

They didn't. He found someone else.

After the weekend when things broke completely, I showed up at the Garcia's with half a heart and puffy eyes. Mercedes looked at me, and she knew. Ava left my weary arms, and Esme greeted her with a smile and a book. Then, Mercedes asked the question that people would be scared to ask for months to come. "Where is he?"

I couldn't answer and just shook my head. Even though I couldn't see it coming, those around me could. And now, just like after he left, I had no idea what I was going to do.

I heard a cry from the other room, and Mercedes stood up.

"I have to cut numbers. Ava can come for the rest of the week to give you time."

She left me sitting there in the quiet to imagine what might have happened here earlier today. I'd heard students describe ICE agents pounding at the door, coming to take loved ones away. There were instructions: don't answer the door, don't answer any questions, and don't allow them to take anyone away. Is that what happened here? Were Esme and Erika okay? I had no answers. My questions would have to wait because Mercedes emerged with Ava in her arms. I took her and held her, warm and soft, still waking up from her nap.

"We'll check in later," I told Mercedes and she nodded. But before the swinging gate could close behind us, Ava reached back toward the house, her head cocked to the side as she looked at me and asked, "Esme?"

I turned away, holding my girl even tighter, leaving the hum of this last unanswerable question hanging in the air.

GHOST OF CENTRAL AVENUE

JOVON C. JOHNSON

The cars that sat idle in Friday afternoon traffic began to fade into the skylight, leaving behind a thin layer of smog that filtered into Phillip's lungs like cheap cigarette smoke. As he inhaled the toxic air and peeled himself from the ground, Phillip felt the ache in his lower back and sharp pains from the blisters on his calloused hands. He dug the dried blood and dirt from his nails, and bit off the splintered corners with the few teeth he had left. The sweltering Southern California heat had begun to blacken the scars on his skin, as the sweat from his forehead stung the corners of his eyes. For most people, panhandling on a street median in one of the busiest parts of Compton would've been considered suicidal, but not for Phillip. He welcomed the companionship of uninsured motorists, and the occasional game of Russian roulette as people tried to knock down his elaborate cardboard signs. Signs that read, "Wife has been kidnapped, I need 99 cents for ransom," "Need $ for drug research," and the current sign, "Please Help Need $$ 4 Beer."

As the latest row of cars lined up at the stoplight, Phillip held up his sign and waited to see if someone would notice. A stern-faced Black man sitting in the passenger seat of an old, rusted Ford Escort waved him over. The stiffness in his leg made the short walk feel like a marathon as he hobbled over to the window and stuck his hand out through the Santa Ana winds. The brisk wind that brushed up against the back of his neck was frigid, like the change that dropped into his hand. Phillip backed away from the car and gave the man his usual gratitude of thanks, a spin, slight bow of the head followed by a wave and a smile.

When the silhouette of the car blended into the city block, he reached into his pocket and felt the crinkled dollars and coins.

"Hopefully, I have enough," he said, pulling his hand from his pocket.

Phillip gazed over the littered concrete for any loose change that may have fallen from his pockets during his displays of gratitude. After picking up a few nickels and pennies, he sat down on the corner of his plastic milk crate, which began to crack and buckle. Finding his balance, he lifted a faded sign that had fallen into the gutter and placed it against the streetlight. His empty stomach began to rumble but it did not ache. It was a pain he had gotten to know all too well through the years. Phillip stretched out his arms and took a deep breath to stop the grumbling, but it only grew worse. So, he stood up, rubbed his stomach, and kicked a brown beer bottle off the curb. Rather than shattering, it rolled down into the bone-dry gutter and got caught in all the rest of yesterday's trash.

"What luck," he said.

Phillip smelled a familiar aroma that emitted from Church's Chicken two blocks away. He could almost taste the warm salted grease and honey on his lips. Picking up the milk crate, he stuffed the signs and his personal belongings inside and crossed the street. On the sidewalk next to a stereo that continuously played Dámaso Pérez Prado was a fruit vendor named Cecilia. She was a short Guatemalan woman, dressed in degraded blue jeans with rips and patches. Phillip always called her "hermanita," which she taught him to say on the first day they met. The way Cecilia danced between the oranges brought a continuous smile to Phillip's face. He appreciated the way she laughed during the scorching-hot days and the way she pushed produce onto unsuspecting motorists with her broken English.

"Hola," Phillip said.

The heavy bags of oranges bashed against Cecilia's knees as she unloaded the van. Her vintage Orange crush soda T-shirt that she thought was a great marketing campaign always amused him, along with her orange-and-black striped Halloween socks.

"Hola," she said with a grin.

He put down the crate next to her van and tried his best to start up a conversation, but Cecilia was too busy worrying about her bags of oranges that sat beneath a wilting palm tree. Without looking to see where he was going, she waved him on his way. Phillip counted the cracks in the concrete and tried his best to kick the pebbles on the ground. This was one of the many ways he kept the intense sunlight off of his face. He cherished each city block with its own unique pattern of broken glass and dark stains covering the pavement and the random pieces of trash swept away from someone's yard. There was something unearthly about the bloodstains that never washed away, the shattered bottles, the empty cigarette cartons, the ripped up overdue bills and personalized greeting cards. All the fragments represented someone's brief moment in the deteriorating neighborhood. To him, the sidewalk was a piece of mosaic art as familiar as the Watts Towers.

As he walked down Central Ave towards Church's Chicken, Phillip was greeted by gang members, drug addicts, and old friends. Some would utter beneath their breath, "What happened to Coach?" while others would size him up to see what kind of a threat he was. As usual, a nod from Phillip would be the beginning and end of each conversation. He walked past Tony's liquors, glanced into Price's barbershop, gazed through the window at M & T Donuts, and sped up past the abandoned empty buildings gutted during the riots. He strolled by the vacant lot that used to be the Compton Swap Meet and ducked into the narrow alley littered with syringes, pill bottles, beer cans, broken condoms, and soiled mattresses.

Phillip tapped the makeshift plywood shelters and listened to the hollow echo in the dilapidated structures spray-painted with graffiti, which housed the drifters, sex offenders, and drug addicts.

"Nothing but an empty shell," he said.

He continued down the alley and exited between two buildings near Church's Chicken, where the smell of chicken and potatoes circulated through the vents. He opened the suctioned door and felt the cool air against his skin. The grease popped loudly in the vats beneath the heat lamps behind the cash registers. The workers yelled out customer orders into the back. The smell made him aware of his rumbling stomach that began to ache, so he stood in line and waited patiently.

"What do you want?" The woman at the register said to the man in front of him.

When it was his turn to order she glanced up and grinned.

"The usual, Coach?" she asked.

Phillip opened his hand, revealing the crumpled bills and change. She reached over the counter and folded his hand into hers. She then pulled two empty cups from under the counter and handed them to Phillip.

"Your money isn't any good here. Go sit down."

He nodded and slid off to the side. Phillip filled one cup with strawberry soda and left the other empty. He sat down at a table next to two large windows overlooking the street and placed one cup in front of him. The empty one, he placed across the table. Several minutes later, an employee set down a tray of his usual order of two pieces of chicken, potato wedges, corn, and a biscuit on the table and then returned moments later with an identical meal, which was placed next to the empty cup.

"Enjoy your meal," he said.

Just then, Phillip felt a sudden drop in temperature around the table. He could almost see his breath in the air. He reached over the table, straightened the napkin, and arranged the plastic utensils on the side of the plate.

"I see you ordered for me."

Phillip glanced up at the woman who stood above the table dressed in a loose pink button-down blouse, blue jeans, and brown leather boots that hugged her calves and captured his attention.

"Lauren …" he mumbled.

Phillip looked into her dark warm hazel eyes as she sat down and pulled on the corner edges of her blouse.

"Are you expecting someone else?"

She brushed the side of his cheek with the back of her hand, pulled the hair out of her face, and inhaled the steam from the corn.

"After all these years, you still don't know what I like to drink," she said.

Phillip shrugged but tears began to well up as he recalled the beauty mark on her left hip, the soft tips of her toes, and the curve of her shoulder blades.

"You're undressing me again, aren't you?" she said.

He shook his head, leaned into the chair, and watched her bite into the crisp wing. Flakes of fried batter dropped into her lap as she licked the salty grease from her fingers.

"Do you remember our first date?" Lauren asked.

Phillip gazed through the window toward two teenagers holding hands. He tried to recall his and Lauren's first date, but all he could remember was the anxiety and nervousness he felt as he stuffed his sweaty palms into his pockets. As the teens walked through the double glass doors, he began to remember the thick Murry's hair grease that melted down his forehead, and how the handle slid between his fingers when he tried to open the door for her. He recalled sitting in the corner debating who had the best record, her Stevie Wonder album, *Songs in the Key of Life*, versus his James Brown record, *The Payback*. He remembered the dryness of his lips and a failed attempt to reach across the table for her hand.

"How many times have we been here?" she asked.

"Every anniversary," he said.

Phillip bit into the hard gristle of the wing. She continued about how they ordered the same meal on the menu every year, and how the new cook experimented with the seasoning messing up the perfect meal.

"Do you remember Daniel?"

He frowned at the thought and took a bite into the buttered biscuit.

"What about our ten-year anniversary?" Lauren asked.

Phillip licked the salt off his fingers, took a sip of his drink and shook his head.

She laughed. "You don't remember bringing Daniel."

He sat back into his chair and thought about his son and all his little quirks.

"I remember he devoured the two large sodas and half my meal, and we had to take turns taking him to the bathroom."

Phillip looked towards the restroom door and grinned at the thought.

"We never did that again," she smiled.

Phillip gazed out onto the sidewalk at a group of kids wearing Little League uniforms. Some carried their baseball gloves under their arms and others tapped their bats against the concrete. The uniforms were soiled by grass, dirt, and blood. Some of the kids had tied the ends of their laces together and slung the cleats over their shoulders, others struck them against the street signs and poles. The music from their radio masked the laughter of a lanky kid who playfully hit a female player in the back of the head with a baseball glove. Phillip laughed at the slap that came from the girl almost immediately, which made the lanky kid cry out in pain. He observed the dried blood that crusted alongside a small scar on the right side of the kid's forehead and the long black ducktail braid of hair pulled through the back of the Pirates baseball cap.

"Daniel?" he said.

* * *

Phillip stared as the girl snuck up from behind, placed her hands on each of his shoulders and shoved him into the window. He could see the enthusiasm in the boy's eyes as he whipped around and chased after her.

"I imagine Daniel would act the same way," Lauren said before biting into a biscuit.

Phillip leaned further against the window to see the direction they were traveling.

"What do you mean?" he said.

"He would've been around the same age."

Phillip packed his meal into a bag that he pulled from underneath the tray. Then he felt along the edges of the table where customers had carved gang signs, love notes, and random names into the hard red plastic. He found his name alongside three others, which he had carved with a knife he found outside in a dumpster. He traced his fingers against the rigid grooves and then staggered towards the door.

"Where are you going?" she asked, wiping her mouth.

"I have to go," he said to the pale image on the glass door.

Phillip felt the cold metal handle brush up against his body as he turned in the direction of the boy and his friends who were now blocks away. He picked up his pace until the ache in his left knee started to feel like a million pins being jabbed into his flesh. So, he limped at a relentless pace all the way up to a streetlight on the corner. There, he used the signpost to hold himself steady as he rubbed the thin jean fabric that covered his knee. Two other groups of kids in uniforms converged on the corner where he stood. They were all headed in the same direction.

"Raymond Park," he said to himself.

Phillip took his time to massage the ache in his knee. He knew where they were going, which was only a couple of blocks away. A number of cars drove by with kids waving from the backseat, making him feel like a spectator of a parade. One car stopped and the driver asked if he needed help; as usual, he waved them on. A part of him wanted a ride, but a larger part of him wanted to be alone to revel in the laughter of the kids who stampeded by. He enjoyed the creaking of old cars rolling over the potholes, and the street noises that made the world come alive in his mind.

As he arrived at the outskirts of the park, the Tragniew Park Pirates were running out onto the field. Parents had gathered around the concession stand to gossip. Children played tag beneath the metal bleachers and around the trees. It was all too familiar of a sight. Phillip rubbed the moisture from underneath his eyes onto his sleeve. He dragged his sore body up to the top of the bleachers, and with a bird's eye view surveyed the field, spotting the Gonzales Park Reds huddled together in their dugout.

Phillip studied the defense on the field. It was the same strategy he used years ago when they won the championship. The players in the outfield shifted closer to the infield, the shortstop floated next to second base, the third baseman played off the bag. Thin polyester uniforms hung carelessly off the player's small frames. They couldn't have been over the age of ten, maybe twelve at most, which was around the same age as Daniel. A few of them even looked like Daniel's old friends.

"I had a feeling you were going to be here," Lauren said, rubbing the back of his neck.

She sat down next to him and pulled a lavender crochet sweater over her shoulders. The same one he bought for her years ago for Christmas, the one he never liked, but it was Daniel who picked it out. It was also Daniel who wrapped it in the cartoon section of the *Los Angeles Times* and said it was from him, Dad, and the baby, even though Lauren wasn't pregnant at the time. She wore it to all the night games as a good luck charm. Occasionally, she would complain about how the cold air seeped through the thin yarn, so on the coldest nights, he packed an extra blanket in the bag, alongside the fruit and sandwiches. Phillip wiped his eyes with a napkin he pulled from his bag and looked out onto the field.

"There!" she said.

He spotted an awkward-looking boy in the on-deck circle who stood and swung the bat like Daniel. He was the same height, complexion, and even had the same wide stance. The brim of his hat curved into a half circle. He swung the worn piece of wood, back and forth in his left hand and dug the tip into the dirt. His stride to the batter's box was a carbon copy of Daniel's and when he looked into the stands, Phillip felt a chill on the back of his neck. He wanted to stand up and cheer like the heavyset man in front of him, who jumped from his seat and shouted, "You can do it, son!"

"Looks just like him, doesn't it?" Lauren whispered into his ear.

"It does," he said.

The pitcher's first throw was a knuckleball, followed by two fastballs.

"Two strikes and a foul ball," Lauren said, leaning on his shoulder.

"Don't worry, he'll get the next one," Phillip said.

On the fourth pitch, he hit the ball behind the defense and held up on third base right in front of the bleachers. Phillip examined the way the boy swayed back and forth, anticipating the go-ahead run. His shoulders tightened along, with his clenched jaw, as he sat on the edge of his seat. The boy inched off the base.

"Your hands are shaking," Lauren said.

Phillip longed for the boy to steal home plate and claim the victory. He wanted to stand against the fence behind home plate one last time and yell till his voice became hoarse. Phillip could no longer watch, so he stared up at the bright lamps that lit the field and tried to estimate the number of moths that were drawn into the 1500-watt bulb. In the brightness he saw an image of Daniel, eyes widening to the sound of the ball striking the bat and then taking off running toward home, each stride longer than the other, the tips of his cleats kicking up dirt behind him. In a cloud of dust, he would appear inches beneath the catcher's mitt, and the umpire would announce with his hands raised, "Safe!"

With his eyes closed, Phillip heard the crowd's roar, the stomping of heels onto the thin metal bleacher, and the fathers' screams.

"He's safe," Lauren said. "He's safe."

Phillip took a deep breath and let the frigid air seep into his lungs. He placed his head onto the bench and, with each roar from the crowd, opened and closed his eyes like a restless wave. The players yelling, "hey batter, batter, swing" was soothing, somewhat melodic, and then it was over.

The stands emptied. Phillip got up and followed not too far behind the crowd. He made his way to the backend of the parking lot and turned one last time to gaze at the empty field. He pictured Daniel on the mound throwing out the first pitch of the game.

Lauren pointed to the sideline. "I used to cheer, right over there," she said.

Phillip nodded.

As the flood lights shut off one by one, the waning crescent moon cast a dim light over the field. The light filled in the dark corners of the dugout and a path to the mound.

Phillip stepped onto the field. "I remember," he said.

Lauren placed her cold hands on his shoulders.

"Do you remember the first baseball he brought home?"

Phillip kicked the dirt off the hard white plastic home plate and noticed a baseball in the grass.

"He was so happy. All he wanted to do was tell his father that he hit a home run," she said.

He picked up the ball and examined the dents in the worn leather.

"It was the only game I missed," he said.

Phillip remembered Daniel running into the backyard and accidently shattering the glass table with a baseball.

"You were with the neighbor," she said.

He recalled disciplining Daniel for his recklessness.

"You were mad about that table."

"I never meant to yell at him like that," Phillip said.

"They called you in for that extra shift at the warehouse."

Phillip gripped the threads of the ball and moved towards the pitching mound.

"You suggested that I should take Daniel to the movies," she said.

Phillip concentrated on the hole in the fence behind home plate. He saw the silhouette of Daniel roll the bat across his shoulders, kick the dirt up with his shoe, and crouch down into the batter's box.

"I wish you would have seen the look on your son's face when that ball went over the fence," she said.

Phillip felt Lauren's cold arms wrapped around his chest and her pregnant belly pressed into the crevice of his back. He wiped the tears from his eyes and hurled the ball towards home plate. In his mind, he heard the hit, the cascade of cheers from the stands, and Lauren's screams from the sideline. Soon after the ball crossed home plate, the image faded and he walked off the field onto the silent street.

The next morning, he returned to the same intersection he sat at every day with a sign he made years ago but had never displayed before. He pulled a small box out for donations, placed it on the corner of the intersection on top of three stacked milk crates, and anchored it with a slab of concrete and a bottle of water. With his back against a One-Way signpost, he slid down and balanced the sign against his knees. He rolled Daniel's home run baseball around the top of his knuckles as an unusual number of cars stopped to put money into his box.

Phillip began to recall everything about that weekend. The time he left the house for the extra swing shift, the Paramount drive-in theater Lauren and Daniel went to, the movie she said they were going to see. He remembered being tired from all the work on the production line. Soldering modules onto circuit boards, correcting the wiring, taking a late lunch to get ahead for a promotion. When he arrived home tired from work, he made himself a snack, turned on the TV, and passed out on the couch. In the morning, he had plans to buy Daniel a new baseball glove and purchase some pink paint for the nursery he had promised to paint. He remembered waking up the next morning with the TV playing Saturday morning cartoons. He assumed Daniel woke up early to watch TV and that, sometime in the night, Lauren had snuck in late after the last movie.

There was a knock at the front door. It was hard to peel himself from the leather couch: his legs hurt and his arthritic hands had swollen overnight. Phillip's eyes began to swell. His chest expanded as he took in a deep breath and rolled the ball as if it were a doorknob. Opening the door that morning, he discovered two Los Angeles sheriff's officers outside. One of them studied the Home Sweet Home mat that Lauren had purchased when they first bought the house. The other glanced over Phillip's shoulder and studied the inside of his home. Both officers offered their condolences at the same time. As the deputies explained his pregnant wife and son were killed in a random drive-by shooting, their voices trailed off like the whisper of a baseball in midair. He could only comprehend the word *killed*, as he plummeted to the ground.

"Lauren … Daniel … My baby …" he said.

Phillip felt the weight of someone's hand press into his back. He looked down at a box filled with money placed in front of him, along with three bags of oranges.

"For you, my friend," Cecilia said, looking at the sign that read, *My family was killed on this corner. Need help. Don't know what else to do.*

A FALSE START

CATIE JARVIS

A version of this story was previously published in *The Secrets We Keep* by Dandelion Revolution Press.

On our way to the abortion clinic, there is an old boxy brown car, flipped and blocking one lane of traffic on the 405. The BMWs, the beat-up Nissans, and everything in-between snake around the Los Angeles highway's curves and move in small increments, together, like a single giant creature. The earthy, dead-tree scent of the joint my boyfriend, Troy, and I shared the night before lingers in the car.

"See, Kat? I told you we needed to leave extra early," he says, one hand on the wheel and the other gently squeezing my thigh.

"Yes, you're always proving yourself right," I reply.

Even with traffic, we will arrive early for my appointment due to Troy's stronghold on time. *A good skill for a father to have.* The thought tightens my throat, but I won't let myself cry.

It's the summer of the Rio Olympic Games. Michael Phelps is adding to his illustrious room of gold in a Scrooge McDuck fashion, and the U.S. Women's Gymnastics Team, led by the superhuman Simone Biles, is about to clinch Team USA's first back-to-back gymnastics championships.

Like the athletes on the world stage, I will always remember this day. I play the Olympic theme song over in my head — those proud trumpets, the brass fanfare. Despite my attempts at distraction, I keep putting my hands onto my belly as if anticipating the pain that will ensue later in the day. I feel bad for the damage, the confusion. My uterus will say, *What the fuck? What am I supposed to do now?* Or, *Damn, I've been literally waiting twenty years to try this shit out, and just when I thought I was going to have my shot …* Or maybe, actually, *Phew! That was about to be a shit ton of work, and I was not looking forward to it.*

∗　∗　∗

The woman performing the ultrasound is young and somber. She inserts a long, wide, heavily lubricated pole into my vagina and searches around with it. A small, square screen, resembling the old Macintosh released the year of my birth, 1984, sits next to me, facing away. This is the hard part. "Do you have to pee?" the woman asks me.

"I always have to pee," I tell her. "But I did just pee in a cup for you."

She laughs a little. "Your bladder is full," she tells me.

"Is that a problem?"

"No."

She probes for a moment more. "I can see the pregnancy," she says.

I like this way of putting it. *The pregnancy.* The term seems right; it is nothing more than that. It is a thing not created, not formed, and not going to be.

"Five weeks and five days," she says.

Five is my favorite number, so I wonder what this means. I took to the number when I was five years old because, at that age, I felt old enough to think, reflect, and decide, but young enough to have everything taken care of for me. At five, I felt there was a guided freedom but feared — correctly — that it would be lost in the following years of life. If I decide to keep *the pregnancy*, I could have a five-year-old in no time. Something about this thought, something about the five weeks and five days, makes me start to cry. I text Troy, who sits outside in the waiting room, so near but so far away.

I say: *I feel sad and alone.*

Troy replies: *What can I do?*

What *can* he do, I wonder. *Get over his commitment issues? Stop pining over younger, bigger-breasted girls on Instagram? Marry me? Be a partner that makes me feel ready to have a child?* I refrain from making these suggestions. I say nothing at all.

The ultrasound woman leaves, and I think for a moment that nothing will be okay. I imagine that I'll soon be bawling on the floor, inconsolable. I imagine that I'll go home to the small, neat apartment by the ocean that I share with Troy, grab a few necessities, and straight-up walk out on my whole life. Fortunately, a nurse practitioner, a Spanish-looking woman in her forties, dressed in bright pink scrubs, comes in like a breath of fresh air.

"You are here at the perfect time," she tells me. "There is nothing yet, just cells. Five weeks will be easy to pass."

She pops the first pill out of its foil and places it in the palm of my hand with a glass of water.

"Take," she says. Asking no questions, passing no judgments. "This makes it stop. No more growing."

I swallow the pill and sigh deeply. The nurse walks across the room to look at my chart. I feel relieved, elated. Everything is manageable. Everything is fine.

"You plan to have a child someday?" she asks.

I nod with assurance. In this moment I feel sure. She scrolls through my chart and does a double take of it and then me.

"How old are you?" she asks.

"Thirty-one."

"No!" she says. She looks at the chart again. I don't think she is putting on an act; people often think I look more like twenty-one than thirty-one. It's even a bit alarming to me. Perhaps if I looked my age, I'd be able to settle more easily into what is expected of me during this phase of my life. Would a bit more body fat, some forehead lines, and eye creases encourage me to grow up, to be ready to have a child, and live a more adult life?

"You do not look thirty," she says definitively. "What's your secret?"

"Yoga, I guess." After I say this, I feel like a Los Angeles cliché. *How did I turn into this? How did I get here? Twenty-one-year-olds have abortions, not thirty-one-year-olds. What's gone so wrong inside of me? Why don't I want a child?*

"Yoga. I need to try this," she says.

I nod, encouragingly.

The nurse explains the next set of pills to me. I will take them within twenty-four hours. I will let them sit in my cheek for a half hour until they dissolve. They will cause my uterus lining to shed. This will cause me a considerable amount of pain for a few hours, maybe a few days, and then it will be over. It all seems rather precise.

I didn't know exactly how it worked before today. I actually thought all abortions had to be surgical, even at a very early stage. No one in my life has ever shared their experience of an abortion with me, at least not in any detail. As I sit in the clinic, on the sticky plastic pedestal, I'm saddened by this. I wonder who I will share this experience with. Will it become a secret that I need to hold in fear of other's differing understandings and judgments?

"Okay," the nurse says, ready to dismiss me. "No tampons. No intercourse. No pools or oceans for two weeks."

"Oceans?"

She looks surprised. Maybe no one in her office has ever exclaimed, "Oceans!" just after having an abortion induced.

"No oceans," she assures me. "Your cervix will be open. We don't want any bacteria getting in there."

"I wish you had told me that before I swallowed this pill!"

I'm shaky, visibly upset. I've been duped. Lied to. Led astray. "I'm going scuba diving this weekend. The trip is all set up and paid for. I finished my certification two weeks ago. I can't cancel!"

"Scuba diving?" she asks. "Isn't it scary under there?"

"A bit scary, but beautiful."

"Supposed to be no exerting yourself. No ocean," she reiterates. "Your cervix will be open."

I try to imagine it, my cervix, open like a gaping mouth. Or is it more subtle than that? Open like the little lips of a fish sucking in the breadcrumbs you throw into a pond. Perhaps if I squeeze my pelvic muscles hard enough, I can close it.

"Is there anything I can do?" I ask, almost in tears yet again.

"Maybe pour some cement between your legs so no water will get in," she laughs, then shakes her head and smiles. She can see I've been spun into a tizzy. "It's okay," she says. "Go at your own risk. It will probably be fine."

The nurse folds up her papers. I watch the way her lips purse, and her face creases at the corners as she goes about her tasks. It is clear she's done this many times. Her hair cascades in soft curls down her back that swing from side to side as she organizes and arranges her departure from the small room. In this moment, I love her the way I once loved my grandmother, fully and without judgment, knowing she would never harm me.

"Good luck and stay young," she tells me. "Yoga and scuba diving," she nods, as if youthfulness is her mission and I've given her the key.

I will likely never see this woman again, but she has granted me two precious gifts: acceptance of my five-week, five-day abortion and permission to go scuba diving. When I return to the waiting room, my face shows more optimism than Troy expected.

He kisses me twice on the lips, then takes my hand, as if I am his child, and leads me out to the parking lot. That song pops into my head about the lime and the coconut, and I sing it quietly on the way to our car.

✳ ✳ ✳

From the clinic, we head to the pier at Hermosa Beach — we've both taken the day off work, so why not enjoy it? We walk onto the pier and happen upon a Los Angeles lifeguard swimming competition. Perhaps they are doing it in honor of the Olympics or, more likely, it's something they do every summer. The lifeguards gallop into the water, unabashedly flailing their arms, to get in as fast as possible. They start a strenuous swim through the breakers and to the other side, where their strokes turn elegant, and then around the red buoy markers.

There was a time I wanted to be a lifeguard, not so that every surfer and tourist on the beach would drool over my bikini body, and not for the noble cause of saving lives. I was drawn to the job because of the regime. I would have liked to be forced to wake up early to jog on the beach, to swim in strenuous currents, to be always ready for the task of pulling a heavy struggling body to shore. I would have liked to spend my days outside, staring at the ocean with purpose.

A few of the contestants are nearing the shore. They ride the waves with aggressive kicks and run haphazardly out of the water and to the red finish line.

"We should do a triathlon someday," I say.

"We surf, we scuba dive, ride motorcycles, hike, travel. There's only time for so many things," Troy states.

A baby is one of the things we've decided we don't have time for.

The breeze on the pier is soft and cool and mixes with the sun to goosebump my arms. I close my eyes and listen to the sounds of the waves crashing on the shore and imagine what it would feel like to dive in, that rush of cold and silence. Whenever I am near water, I want to be inside it.

"Are we hungry?" Troy asks. The coordination of our eating is something that he hates about being in a relationship. That we have to decide what and when to eat — together — is a burden he bears more heavily than a person ought to.

"Sure," I say. "Let's eat now before I feel too sick to."

We sit on a small outdoor patio in the shade at a restaurant near the pier. Sitting beside us are three women in their sixties, maybe a little older than our parents, chatting about the Olympics as they share a bottle of some bubbly rosé.

"And that poor French sprinter," one woman says. She has short dark hair recently teased at a beauty parlor. She takes a sip of her drink, and her lipstick leaves its pink print on the glass. "Just one flinch and his dreams of Olympic glory are destroyed," she says. "What a heartbreak!"

"What do you think about that new rule?" her friend asks. She has long earrings made of abalone or something equally pearlescent. They dangle almost touching her slightly lifted shoulders.

"It's not fair!" the third woman says strongly. She is the one who has most clearly had work done on her face. Maybe a lift; certainly collagen fillers. "It's not right!"

They are talking about Wilhem Belocian. They are talking about the false start rule initiated in 2010 that no longer gives racers one warning if they jump the gun but, instead, enforces immediate disqualification.

"They are the top athletes in the world," Abalone Earrings says. "They must be held accountable. There is no room for error at this level of the game."

"Games!" Teased Hair exclaims. "The Olympics are just a bunch of games. We are not robots, and we all err sometimes."

They are talking about the 110-meter hurdle race on Monday night, two days past. I'm not a track enthusiast, and as a former gymnast, I mostly watch the summer Olympics to indulge my old passion. But on that Monday night, my eyes had filled with tears as Belocian paced the track with his hands on his head after he realized what he had done. After all his training. One preemptive move and it was all over. He unzipped his blue and red costume, separating the letters FRA from the NCE across his chest, and crumpled to the ground.

At the time, I didn't find it particularly odd that I had cried. Perhaps, in hindsight, I had been more emotional due to the hormones pumping through my system. I have a special empathy for people in those moments when they let themselves down in our already harsh and unforgiving world. When they do things that can never be undone.

"He'll lay in bed every night for the rest of his life regretting that moment," the third woman says, with her tightly pulled back cheeks that don't let on how much she feels. "We are too hard on ourselves," she continues. "I've learned that much."

I wonder how these women have come to know each other. How long they have lived in Los Angeles. How long they have all been friends. They must have each lived many different lives by now, phases of their human experience. I wonder if any of them has had an abortion. And if they ever spoke of it.

"I wonder what we'll be like at that age," I whisper to Troy.

"Old, babe. Old," he says. I can tell by the dullness in his green-gray eyes that he doesn't imagine us together at that age. He is not the grow-old-with-me type. What is a girl to do when she's thirty-one and in love with the type of man who can't speak of forever?

My rather large steak, tomato, and avocado baguette arrives like a challenge set out before me. "I'm going to do my best to eat the whole thing," I tell Troy. "Because I'm sure that I won't have an appetite later."

"Have at it!"

As I reach for my sandwich, he intercepts my hand across the table and holds it. "I've got you," he says. And he does.

✳ ✳ ✳

When we get home to our one-bedroom apartment in Santa Monica that we can barely afford, Troy sits with me while the pills turn chalky in my cheek. We watch *Million Dollar Listing Los Angeles*, our guilty pleasure, and imagine that we live in a modern turnkey on the sea in Malibu and sleep in a bedroom with floor-to-ceiling windows looking right out on the waves.

"Babe, if only there were a dry beach," he says.

"We can live with a wet-dry for now. We'll just suntan when the tide is down," I reply.

When the pain hits me hard, Troy has a bowl of weed ready and supplies steady doses of painkillers with lightly buttered cinnamon toast so that I won't throw up. He rubs my shoulders as I rock back and forth on my knees on the living room floor, and he says that he's sorry.

I know that he can't understand this pain, but I want him to. "It feels like it's so deep inside," I tell him. "It's a constant stomachache, and it's radiating like a broken bone; it's burning like a hot stone pushed into the skin. It's everything, all at once."

He draws me a hot bath, and though I'm hesitant, I try it. Once I submerge, my body stops convulsing, everything relaxes.

"This really feels amazing," I tell him with tears in my eyes. "You know, my grandmother tried to abort my mother by taking a hot bath."

I lay my head back onto the hard edge of the tub.

"Is that a thing?"

"Well, back then, it was like something women said could work. Anyway, it didn't work for her, obviously."

He leans back and pushes himself up to sit on the sink counter. "Why'd she try to do it?"

"She was bipolar, and her pregnancies brought on bad episodes. She didn't want to go through it again."

"Babe!" he shouts. He points at the tub with a horrified glare.

A bloody chunk shaped like a tiny tongue lingers between my legs. Around it, swirls of blood spiral toward the surface of the water. He's surely imagining that it's our aborted child. For some reason, I laugh.

"It's my uterus lining and some blood," I say matter-of-factly. "It looks that way with my period sometimes too; it's fine." *Just cells. Five weeks and five days.*

After the bath, he walks with me to the bed, holding my hunched and aching body. He gets my heating pad, another half a painkiller, and a glass of whiskey with ice, which I sip before I drift off to sleep. He checks on the heating pad for me during the night to make sure that it's safe and not too hot, as it is old with a frayed wire. It belonged to my grandmother, now dead ten years, and I refuse to get a new one so long as it still works. I imagine she must have clutched its yellow flowered print to her own stomach many a time, wishing away the pains of her life.

* * *

When I tell my best friend Betty about the abortion over the phone the following morning, she says, "What has become of us when we care more about scuba diving trips than the prospect of bringing a life into the world?"

This is not offensive because the "we" refers to her and me. We are in this thing together now. We are the kind of women who are in their thirties but aren't married with 2.5 children, a house and at least two types of acceptable pets. She calls us "outside cats" and no longer believes we'll ever properly fit societal norms. She thinks we've gone too far, seen too much, thought too hard, lost any affinity we may have had toward "normalcy." I'm not totally sure I agree with her. Nor do I disagree.

"But I'll be fine, right?" I ask her. "If I go for the dive? I'm not risking my safety in a real way, am I?" I'm looking for her vote of confidence, which is usually easily won.

"It's basically a bad period from this point out," Betty assures me. "You passed the hard part. Everyone's just covering their asses."

I'm walking down Montana Avenue towards the ocean. The street is populated with well-off white women and their small dogs, expensive clothing stores, coffee shops, and perfectly spaced trees. I talk quietly so that no one might know what I am discussing, what I have done.

"You know what cracks me up?" she asks.

"What?"

"The whole dichotomy of the thing. Like, if you're keeping the baby, you immediately stop doing anything dangerous or putting anything bad into your body. You run to the nearest health food store to purchase high-quality prenatal vitamins, you throw out all the coffee, alcohol, and high fructose corn syrup, and you immediately do as many sets of bun burners and crunches as humanly possible, knowing that your body isn't going to look like it does now ever again. Whereas, if you're not going to keep the baby ..." She takes a well-timed pause. "Upon seeing the two blue lines, you immediately have a drink, smoke a bowl, drive to the clinic, where a bunch of terrible chemicals go in your body. All the while, your poor, confused reproductive system, which has finally been activated on the most complex and insane task ever imaginable — growing a human life — is suddenly shocked to a halt. The proverbial alarms sound. The green light turns unexpectedly red."

"A false start," I say.

"Exactly!" she replies.

"Maybe you should make that some kind of standup act," I suggest to her.

She chuckles hard.

I flash a brief smile into my phone but quickly grow sad, thinking about the fact that she's had two abortions. I know nothing about her procedures, really, except that they were had. We never discussed what her experiences were like, how she felt during or after, or since. No details, lessons, or emotions. What kind of friends did that make us? Was this lack of sharing due to her shame or was it my failing for not asking questions? I want to tell every person that I consider a friend every detail of what my abortion was like, about every strange sensation flooding through me. I want to tell them so that they never have to feel it's something that can't be discussed or shared. I open my mouth to begin some sort of confession, but Betty cuts in before I have the chance to get anything out.

"To be honest …" she begins, and I think for a moment that she's going to offer something profound, real, and true to make it all make sense. But all she says is, "I'm more worried about the sharks than anything else. Is it true that menstrual blood attracts sharks? You be careful down there. Please don't get eaten, I couldn't bear it."

"I won't get eaten," I assure her, "and, no, menstrual blood does not attract sharks any more than urine or a tiny cut on your cuticle. That's just another thing that women are told to make them feel afraid, compromised." We exchange quick goodbyes, and my chapped-lips seal closed in the California sunshine.

✳ ✳ ✳

Anacapa Island pops volcanic brown against the crisp blue of the sky and the Pacific. The expansive rock rises out of nowhere in the middle of the ocean, and even when you are right up beside it, it hardly seems real. It is the second smallest of the Channel Islands in Ventura County, at about five miles long. Fittingly, Anacapa means mirage.

Our dive boat, *The Explorer*, rocks back and forth as we make our way. Troy holds my waist as we rise and fall together at the ocean's will. The day is so clear that it is unnerving. I feel like I'm on the set of a movie with a convincingly fake island backdrop behind me. Troy is the love interest lead, the good-looking man who will neither break up with nor settle down with the devoted protagonist. I think, *What silly dramas we play out in this life.*

The ride out to the Channel Islands is two hours and requires Dramamine even for those not normally cursed with seasickness. On my first trip out, when I didn't take any, the sensation was almost exactly like the one bout of morning sickness I woke up with, which had alerted me to "the pregnancy" in the first place. It's been three days, and all my pain from the abortion has ceased. I have taken my Dramamine, and I feel fine. The whole ordeal is behind me. The only thing I have left to worry about is putting on my thick wetsuit and gearing up with weights, tank, BCD, hoses, gloves, boots, fins, and mask. Oh, and the tampon that I'm not supposed to be wearing to withhold my still heavy bleeding, and the lingering anxiety about entering the ocean with an open cervix.

When all my gear is on and tested, I hold my face-mask with one hand and my regulator with the other, jumping fins first off the boat. Once the water absorbs the weight of all the gear — and I pass the initial anxiety of descending — my mask tightens to my face, my ears equalize, and my body relaxes toward the bottom of this patch of ocean.

Everything becomes vivid and present, the way all life should be.

I touch the sandy bottom and look around to orient myself. The anchor of *The Explorer* hooks the ocean floor behind me, and ahead there's nothing but kelp forest, rock crests, and fish. I hold my hands still and maintain my buoyancy. The fish don't seem to mind me. A deep-orange Garibaldi swims up, its beady black eyes meeting mine. Troy floats nearby; he's a bright blue and yellow creature inhabiting this strange world as easily as he inhabits the one above. I give him the okay sign to let him know I'm doing well, and he pulls out his air for a moment to blow me a dramatic kiss. This is my first "real" dive, unaccompanied by an instructor, since my recent certification course. It feels like freedom to wander this underwater world.

The water takes hold of me. The breeze above turns to tides below, and the kelp trains sway gently from side to side with me, everything under the water dancing silently together. There are innumerable coral puffs in fluorescent purple and pink. In its secret rock world, there's a lobster hiding in the shadows, upright and alert like an old man in a doorway, like my own father so often on the lookout for visitors or intruders on the dead-end New Jersey street I grew up on. I wonder what my father would think of my abortion. He never judged me harshly, almost incapable of seeing my flaws, but I think it would have made him sad that there could have been a new life born from me, into the world. Perhaps if he were still alive and could meet my child, I would feel differently about having one. I hope someday to feel the call of motherhood the way I feel the call, in this moment, toward the bottom of the sea. But if I don't, that's okay too. At least there *are* things in this world that call to me. For this, I am grateful.

I listen to the sound of my oh-so-human inhales and exhales, oozing loudly in and out of the second stage of my regulator like deep yoga breaths. I enjoy the feeling of the water surrounding me and nothing more — no industry, no smokestacks, housing developments, or storefronts advertising this or that. No people walking briskly with downturned eyes. No noises of life, of motorcycles, music, voices, or sirens.

I feel once again "wombed" — completely submerged, breathing underwater through a cord. I was once an unformed being inside a watery organ, a place I outgrew and exploded forth from. In the same way, I will someday have outstayed my welcome on earth and vanish to another unknown. The whole cycle of life seems to make sense down here. I wish that I could show this place to the nice nurse in the bright pink scrubs.

Sunlight slices the water above in majestic lines. I take a deep inhalation of my dry oxygen and exhale bubbles that grow and float above me like a cluster of translucent jellyfish glistening in the light. I want to cry because I feel closer than ever before, not to "the pregnancy," a group of cells, but to a someday-soul submerged deep within myself — a great and beautiful possibility that, at forty feet under, I can almost align with, I can almost believe in and understand.

RIDING THE BLUE LINE

MARY ANNE PEREZ

Tula rarely considers herself lucky to work an hour from home at a corporate job where the managers brush past her on the way to their remodeled offices. Her greetings of "Good morning" or "How ya doing?" dissolve into the white noise of the office, rarely answered.

After another long day, she takes a deep breath and trudges toward the Blue Line that will take her home, down the Bunker Hill steps and quickly through the library that always smells brand new. She tries to remember the gratitude prescribed by motivational icons, whom she watches online late at night, as she walks down Flower and sidesteps the swirl of possibly human shit on the sidewalk next to the library.

On 6th Street, she's grateful that she sees only the aftermath of the suicide from the Standard's rooftop bar, covered in a white sheet. She looks up, counts seven stories.

She thinks of the person's mother and of her own teenage son and tries to cast out the horror that's befallen this stranger. She's grateful she hadn't been in a car that afternoon when whoever it was could no longer take it and decided on making a final leap. A stranger murmurs, "Dude jumped."

As she crosses the street, she looks toward the matte-black coroner's van.

Today, a rare rain pummels the city, and she's grateful to find a seat on the train heading to Long Beach. The door-closing warning is barely audible over the din of the crowded car. The drenched passengers close their umbrellas, shake off droplets from their slick jackets, slide back their hoods, and settle in for the ride home. Some rest their heads on the grimy windows, too tired to care about what's left behind.

As the train heads from the tunnel toward Pico station, Tula hears a faint strumming and notices a young man in the seat in front of her with a ukulele resting in his arms. He wears a beret, and a short braid of dark brown hair appears from under the hat. His jacket is folded next to him over his backpack and he's sitting at an angle, taking in the range of humanity gathered on a shared mission to reach home.

The aisles are clogged with passengers holding onto backpacks, purses, diaper bags, and strollers; one holds an infant, another holds bags of soda and beer cans and plastic bottles to be recycled. Those who stand hold onto the backs of seats or the metal bars on the ceiling that run along the length of the car, gripping tightly as each stop throws them off balance.

The hum of conversation flows, and Tula makes out the languages among the mixture of voices sounding alert, happy, or angry. She closes her eyes in meditation and exhaustion. The pull of a paycheck has kept her too long in a job that holds silent disdain for her, where she endures whispers and glances of her coworkers when she enters the office. She will not tell anyone how much she relates to the jumper, and how she fantasizes about her last shot of Patrón (or maybe an expensive whiskey) and that last leap of faith.

She listens to friends, students, and coworkers chatting and laughing. The shrill, long beep when the doors open and close is an oppressive reminder this crowd doesn't need, that luxury is not reserved for them, even though their toil has paid for the seats they occupy. They're not afforded the comforts of the quieter, cleaner, more spacious MetroLink that takes commuters to the less crowded and noisy suburbs of the L.A. Basin, where people don't live on top of each other or hear the nightly buzz of helicopters. On MetroLink, the approaching stops are announced by a soothing bell, friendly and happy. On MetroLink, the seats are cushier and the aisles wider. On MetroLink, there are hooks for bicycles and racks overhead for bags. Once Tula took it to visit her cousin in Covina and half expected a gloved porter to appear, a cloth draped over his forearm, serving cappuccinos from a tray held expertly on one hand. No jostling with sweaty students and weary service workers after long shifts of bussing tables and cleaning toilets. The Blue Line, on the other hand, snakes through South Los Angeles, Watts, and Compton.

She notices vendors slip up and down the rows after every stop, beneath the pervasive smell of smoky, skunky weed. They're selling a surprising array of things you may need on a long commute: bottles of cold water, soda, candy, earphones, socks, chips. They roll their carts and ice chests up the aisle, set their goods down, and make their pitch. Hustlers all.

"Five dollah, five dollah, five dollah," barks a young man, a rainbow of earphones draped over his shoulder as he squeezes through the standing crowd. He reminds her of the plomeros and landscapers who post neon-colored notices along Slauson and Manchester that cover telephone poles, looking like confetti in Mark Bradford's collages that hang in The Broad, and of the men and women who stand on street corners selling bouquets of wilting flowers and sacks of oranges.

The weary commuters on the train make space for the hustlers, respectful of the societal notch where they reside, mindful of their own notch in life as office workers, bank tellers waiting to transfer closer to home, construction crews with their safety vests grimy from the day's work. At least these passengers are headed home, unlike the hustlers still clocking in as people reach their stop along the way.

Today, the beeps and skunky smells are accompanied by regular announcements that the Blue Line will no longer be the Blue Line and the Green Line will no longer be the Green Line and the Gold Line will no longer be the Gold Line. The lines are losing their colors and changing to an efficient system of A, B, C. Even in this land where people come to dream, someone in the marble Metro tower has decided that there must be order. Tula had hoped to one day ride the Chartreuse Line and transferring to the Magenta Line to connect with cousins riding on the Indigo Line, but that's not to be. She resigns herself to never seeing an artist's depiction of the trains changing color and design when they enter different neighborhoods: murals for East Los Angeles, firecrackers for Chinatown, stars for Hollywood. She overheard the idea at a cocktail party in the warehouse district in the nineties. An artist's dream, or was it her own? It was so long ago now.

Letters are easier to see on maps than the color names, the announcements say. Except there won't be an "H" line because that letter is universal for Hospital. There won't be an "I," which stands for Information. And there won't be an "F," something about not trusting the masses not to add "uck" at every station.

"That's some bullshit," a young man exclaims to no one and everyone around him. "Man, how're they going to make that work?" He looks around for support and finds a few nodding heads. "In L.A., of all places, they want us to go back to A, B, C? I'm just going to keep calling this the Blue Line, and they can call it whatever the fuck they want."

Tula wonders where an F line would run anyway. In Tula's experience, sometimes after a long, hard day the entire system can feel like a big fat F: Failure, Futility, Floundering. Flunking out of the life she really wants, stuck in a dead-end job. Some days as she's headed home, she realizes how Fucked her life has become.

Sometimes.

Other times, more often really, she witnesses small miracles and servings of grace. Once she heard an argument between two L.A. Trade Tech students as they stood near the sliding doors a few rows behind her. Their argument, loud and accusatory, got more forceful, and she dreaded what would come next. It was something about one of them spitting too closely to the other. They disputed the facts. Each man stood up for himself, and then they slowly simmered down until one of them said he didn't mean to spit at the other guy but wasn't paying attention. He apologized.

A man sitting next to Tula leaned over to her. "Are you hearing this?"

They both smiled at the phenomenon of witnessing an almost-fight turn into a handshake.

Once on the Green Line, when she was working in El Segundo, Tula saw a large, tatted-up man give up his seat for an abuela, insisting that she sit despite her protests. Tula looked his way with a smile, hoping to catch his gaze. She wanted him to see her nod of approval, but he stared straight ahead until she got up to leave. Another day, a man playing classical guitar got on the train in North Long Beach and played his music. Just him and his guitar. Nobody seemed to know him, but that wasn't unusual. Tula guessed that he was practicing for a concert. He had a certain refinement about him, and his music seemed to clean the air. He exited at Rosa Parks, still playing his guitar.

Another journey, a family of musicians crowded the center aisle before starting a rough melody that Tula vaguely remembered her aunt and uncle requesting from the mariachis in Puerto Nuevo. The family band was led by the father, who was told by the conductor not to ask for money on the train. But as the official repeated his warning, passengers' hands shot up holding dollar bills for the family, like a protest in motion. Don't tell closed-in passengers not to support each other, especially when someone wants to sing or play an instrument.

Sometimes it's just too much, like when some people refuse to turn down their loud boomboxes, despite pleas from fellow travelers who are brave enough to broach the subject. One time, Tula asked a young man if he didn't have earphones because his music was too loud. He was standing right next to where she was seated, and he surprised her by apologizing and silencing his phone. Tula wondered where that earbud salesman was when she needed him.

She's seen money and wild applause given to young men who recite redemption poems from memory. A couple of other times, she's heard the same poem but from different young men, following the same pattern, the same verses, and receiving the same love and appreciation. A scam or an organized circle raising funds for something? How much of the take do the young men get to keep? It didn't matter much to the passengers because, after a long day, these words bring some peace and healing and lift weary spirits, even if they are only rehearsed lines hawked in a crowded train for money.

One year, as she and her fifteen-year-old son rode the Blue Line north into DTLA for the New Year's Eve party at City Hall, a chatty young hustler rolled his ice chest toward her, calling out, "Sodas! Water! Gatorade! Candy! And for New Year's, cerveza, tequila, cigarettes!"

Now he had everyone's attention and continued, "Modelo! Corona! Hornitos! Patron!"

There were more than a few takers.

He then rolled his ice chest to where two cars meet in a swerving compartment, where the cameras wouldn't see him, and he would know: he had been cited many times before, he said.

On this rainy day after the long workday, when the passengers are grateful for shelter and to be going home, the ukulele player in front of her quietly strums as the train makes its way south. At each stop, the doors release more passengers. Compton, Artesia, Del Amo. As the din of the crowd diminishes, she can hear the soft strums more clearly.

A man wearing a thin T-shirt, his hair a tangled mess, sits three rows ahead and stares back at the musician. He nods at him in thanks, a slight smile forming. When the train is almost empty, he looks at the ukulele player and says, "Man, that does something to me."

He touches his chest and says again, "Your music does something to me. I needed to hear that today."

The young musician stops his strumming and asks the man what is going on. The weary man tells him his clothes are soaked through and he doesn't have anything to change into.

The musician puts his ukulele down and reaches into his backpack.

"Could you use some socks?" he asks.

Surprised, the drenched man nods, and the musician pulls out a pair of C-Line green socks that are folded into a tight ball. They could have been straight out of the dryer and folded ready for a dresser drawer, but he has them in his backpack. Tula wonders if he does this often or if the socks are just something he happens to have on him today.

He hands the socks to the grateful man and rises to leave. They are in Long Beach now, and Tula's stop is near. The rain has lessened to a light drizzle.

Tula thinks of impermanence.

As she rides the train every day and walks to and from the office and to and from her home two blocks from the last stop, she realizes that everything — this train ride, the rain, her shitty job, yes, all of it will end one day. Any relief that comes from that thought is diminished by the counter thought, that everything good — these beautiful gestures among humans cramped on a train, an airy guitar riff, the generosity of passengers each struggling in their own right — is temporary too. Her son's teen years, her lifelong friendships, her family, her siblings and their families, her dog, and her dreams will pass one day as well. It all ends. All of it, herself included. There's something about remembering that we're all grains of sand, dust to dust, that makes it easier to appreciate everything in its place.

THE BETTER SISTER

TIARA ITO

Two hours ago, I got a call from my sister.

"Wake up, Big Head. We're going shopping!"

Kenya's voice was high-pitched in my ear. I closed my laptop, not wanting to look at the job postings that mocked me. They were all the same. Minimum pay for mediocre work, all because I thought an English degree was a good idea. *You should've done engineering like your big sister*, I could hear my mom say. Never missed a beat to let me know where I went wrong. The music from my sister's car blasted through the phone.

"Didn't Carl tell you no more shopping sprees? Besides, now isn't a good time," I said.

Lately, it was never a good time for anything. It had been three weeks since I was laid off as a bank clerk, and I still had no luck finding the next gig.

She laughed, and I could sense her eyeroll through the phone. Carl. When it came to that man, she never took him seriously. They were college sweethearts and have remained together ever since. I always wondered what he saw in her, but in his eyes, Kenya could do no wrong.

"Please, you know that man ain't leaving me. Besides, this shopping trip is for you, not me," she said.

My ears twitched at the words. "And why do I need this again?"

"Because, Nettie, life is too short to be cooped up in a dingy apartment crying over a job. You need to live a little, girl. Be more like your big sister."

Irritation flared in my chest. No matter what we talked about, the conversation always went the same. It always ended with a comparison between us, and there was no surprise about who came out on top. I sucked in a deep breath and tried to practice that "mindful breathing" I learned about on NPR. I could refuse her offer, but I knew my sister. Even if I said no, it'd only be a matter of time before she was at my door, banging it in or kicking it down.

I got up and walked over to my dresser, making sure to avoid my reflection in the mirror as I passed it. "Can you at least tell me where we're going so I can look somewhat decent?" Knowing Kenya, she would be dressed up like she was about to attend NY Fashion Week.

There was a pause on her end as she contemplated telling me. It's a mystery how my eyes didn't fall out of my head from rolling them so hard. The seconds dragged on until I snapped, "Kenya!" My outburst was only met with laughter. A strong, resonating sound that echoed off the walls of her car. I caught a glimpse of myself smiling in the mirror. Her deep laughter always infected me. I wiped the smile away.

"Alright, alright. Loosen up, will you?" she said between laughs. "I'm taking you somewhere that you're going to love." She went quiet again, and there was a pause between the music.

"And that is?"

I could sense her smile through the phone. "Don't worry, you'll see."

* * *

Fifty minutes later, Kenya and I approached the store's entrance. And as predicted, she looked like a model. Her long braids Rapunzeled down the length of her back with the top half twisted into a bun. She kept her nails trimmed to mid-length but with enough room to paint vibrant sunflowers on them. On her wrist, dangled a gold bracelet that sparkled in the sun. It slid freely up and down her forearm and looked one gesture away from slipping off. On the other hand, I looked like her bumbling sidekick. I wore old jeans that fit well enough, my worn-out Brown University sweatshirt, and small locs that were still waiting to mature.

A red neon sign blazed in the window, and the place didn't seem like much from the outside. Large stone slabs scaled their way up the exterior walls, like every other office building on the block. It had wide, tall glass windows filled with the store's name and glimpses of the inside.

People walked past us — some tourists, some locals — and it hit me that I had never explored the city. I lived in L.A. for almost three years but spent most of that time working or chasing after failed dreams. When I graduated from Brown, I thought I'd make it big like my sister, who had it easy from the moment she left campus. A nice six-figure salary as a software engineer at Microsoft, plus a luxury apartment with a view. Failure wasn't in the equation for her. For me, it wasn't the same. I struggled to find work as a screenwriter from the moment I landed at LAX and had to settle for odd jobs ever since. Kenya offered to let me stay with her and Carl, but things weren't so bad that I'd stoop to asking her for help. I told her I'd manage things on my own, but now where was I? Back again at the bottom, while Kenya got to look down on me from the top.

"You ready?" Kenya asked, pulling me out of my thoughts. She was looking at me with her eyebrow raised, and I would recognize that look anywhere. She placed her hand on my arm and squeezed, but I pulled it away. I tried to give her a small smile to reassure her instead, but again, that look was there. The one that sees through me as if I'm made of glass. I walked toward the door, hoping to free myself from her gaze, but a man in a dark hat rushed past me, barging into me, almost knocking me to the ground.

"Watch it, asshole!" Kenya yelled after him, but the man hurried down the street with his head down until he disappeared.

"Are you alright, Nettie?" Kenya was beside me, her concerned eyes searching my body for damage. I told her I was fine so she wouldn't make a scene, but my arm pulsated underneath my sleeve. Kenya was always the confrontational one. She was never afraid to use her voice whenever and however she wanted, and it was a quality of hers I envied. I still remember how she dragged two boys off the bus in the fifth grade when she found out they were bullying me. Seeing my sister yell at a bunch of kids like she was my mother was mortifying, but then, those boys never bothered me again. Thinking about that memory, I should've felt a sense of gratitude for her. But at the time, it only made me feel small. As if that moment was another reminder of how I couldn't measure up and do what came so naturally for her.

My arm throbbed again where the man had hit me, but I brushed it off with a wave. "I'm fine," I said, shaking my arm. "He's probably looking for a toilet."

My sister laughed, and surprisingly, I found the sound soothing. The pain in my arm dulled, and I motioned toward the door. "Now, can we go in?" I said, wanting to change the subject. Kenya wrapped her arm around me and pulled me in close. I stiffened under her hold.

"This is gonna blow your mind," she said with a smile.

* * *

I don't know what I was expecting. Maybe a few books here and there with an old store manager at the register, but nothing spectacular. When we walked through the entryway, it was like an entire world opened up. The space was double the size I thought it would be. There was a record store attached to the left of the building, plus two floors of endless books. I looked up at the high ceiling, and it felt like I was in the library version of the Sistine Chapel. Kenya put her fingers on my chin and closed my mouth.

"You're drooling." She winked.

I would've said something smart back to her, but the words weren't there. Instead, I was in complete awe. Since this was a place Kenya picked out, I assumed it'd be something more to her tastes than mine. However, I was surprised to see she picked a place that was perfect for me.

We walked deeper into the store, and Kenya started pointing out sections to me. At one point, she picked up a fantasy book and asked if I had ever finished the series. I read it in middle school, so I was surprised to see that she still remembered. I said no but held onto the book because it stirred something familiar in me. We continued, and she kept bringing up moments from our childhood that I had long forgotten. She talked about how I used to only read romance novels in the backyard and how whenever I read a mystery novel, I'd run around the house trying to solve fake crimes. In the end, I would determine that she was always guilty, even though she never knew what her crimes were.

While I listened to her, I was impressed that she could remember everything about me with such clarity. I had always assumed that no one else had noticed me back then. But after hearing her speak, it made me wonder if that assumption was true. When she spoke of me, there was a light in her eyes that I hadn't seen before that made me feel flustered. She didn't look like the old Kenya to me. It was like my vision of her had been adjusted.

✳ ✳ ✳

By the time we reached the second floor, I had already amassed a collection of books that I was struggling to carry. Kenya laughed as I added another to my pile.

"Girl, you better slow down before you break those twigs you call arms. You haven't been hitting the gym that hard." She grabbed three books off the top of my pile and held them. "I think they have some tote bags for you to carry these in. Wait there, and I'll bring you one."

She motioned her head in the direction of a bench that was in the corner of the history section. I placed the rest of the pile on the bench. Kenya started to walk off but turned around after two steps, and said, "And don't you add another book to that pile until I get back."

My fingers were already on the spine of another book. I pulled my hand away and gave a slight nod. She was more perceptive than I thought. I added that to the list of "Kenya Surprises" for the day. I listened to her heels clack down the hall as she headed toward the stairs.

In my corner of the store, it was quiet. Some people passed by and looked at the shelves, but even with people coming and going, I discovered a sense of ease. The sound of two young girls caught my attention, and I followed their trail of voices. The trail led me around a corner, and I found myself at the opening of a tunnel created by stacks of books on the left and right that curved their way up the walls and ceiling and met in the middle to create a perfect archway. The two girls, about ten years old, stood in the center and pointed at the string lights above their heads. They spread their arms out wide, as if under a starry sky, and spun in circles. Their laughter filled the space, and after a few more turns, they grabbed each other's hands and ran off.

I took a step forward and stood in the middle of the book tunnel. There was no one around me, so I closed my eyes and spread my arms the same way I had seen the two girls do. I smiled to myself. Being there made me feel like a kid again, like the little girl my sister told me about from our childhood. The one who didn't feel like her life was hopeless but saw a world of endless possibilities instead. The one who didn't mind spending a little time with her older sister, even though, one day, that would change.

Before, when I would think of Kenya, there was a piece of hot coal in my stomach. Whenever someone mentioned her name, a fire was stoked and I would find myself burning with resentment over the person I could never be. I could never match her wit, beauty, or accomplishments, so it made sense that I held her as the one to blame. But the longer I stood there trying to recall when she was cruel or unjust, I found the memories didn't exist. She was always kind when she didn't need to be, but that didn't fit the villain I demanded for my story. Instead, there was an image of her I had painted that I was desperate to uphold.

A hint of lavender brushed over my senses as a person walked by, and I was reminded of my sister's favorite scent — Amazing Grace by Philosophy. My smile grew wider, and another image of Kenya flashed into my mind. We were kids again, and I was standing at the end of our street block, waiting to be picked up after school. I searched back and forth for that familiar face in the crowd of parents arriving to pick up their kids, and when I saw her, I didn't hesitate to grab onto her hand. Yes, I could see it now. How I was always searching and waiting for Kenya to come to me. I remembered the joy I felt walking home from that bus stop, hand in hand with her like the two girls I had just seen.

I pictured my sister again, but this time, I saw the light in her eyes when she talked about me. The place in my stomach where I used to feel fire toward her started to change. The new sensation still had a warmth to it, but it was coupled with an unfamiliar feeling that I couldn't explain. I sat with the feeling until it became so clear that I had no choice but to name it — Love. Love so deep and unconditional that it seeped through my veins.

* * *

A woman cleared her throat behind me, and I opened my eyes. A line had gathered while I stood in the middle of the tunnel. I gave an apologetic bow before I headed back to my section.

On my way back, I tripped over a dark duffle bag that had been left on the floor. I caught myself before I toppled into the shelves. Annoyed, I kicked the bag away with my foot. Who leaves a bag in the aisle anyway? I returned to my book pile and found Kenya waiting for me. She tapped her foot and gave me the universal big sister look that screamed, "*Where the hell have you been?*" But seeing her only made the emotions in me grow stronger. I walked up to her and hugged her, and her body stiffened under my sudden affection.

"Uh, who are you, and what have you done with my sister?" she asked.

I looked up at her with a smile; it was the first time I wanted to kiss her. I puckered up and placed one on her cheek. She pushed me off in surprise. "Girl, what has gotten into you? Did you bump your head or something?" The look on her face was priceless.

"I just missed you, that's all." I went back for a hug, and she palmed my forehead, keeping me at a distance. She eyed me up and down.

"Somebody slip you a drug or something?"

I almost choked on my laughter. "I'm just trying to say thank you!"

Her eyes widened, and she dropped her hand. "Thank me for what?" She still had her guard up, but I could tell she was genuinely interested.

"You were right," I said. "This was exactly what I needed."

And then, the light in Kenya's eyes grew brighter.

We piled my books into the tote bag she had brought me and continued our walk around the second floor. Now that things felt different, I found that there was so much more I wanted to say to her. It was like I needed to speak for all the years I missed. I told her about the things I wanted to do and the person I wanted to become, and she listened. She allowed me to share what I needed, and I appreciated every second of it.

We made our way to the register, and by the time I reached the front of the line, I had accumulated more books and shared more dreams than one person could probably handle. But Kenya didn't judge me. She simply laughed, patted my shoulder, and said she was proud of me. She helped me unload my books onto the counter.

"That'll be $212.30," the cashier said.

Kenya whipped out a card from her purse and looked at me with a mischievous smile. "We'll charge this to Mr.

Carl's account." She slid it across the counter to the girl, who accepted it with a knowing look.

The cashier swiped the card in her system and handed it back with a grin. "Enjoy your day, ladies. And don't forget to thank Carl for us."

We both laughed, and it felt good to connect with my sister again. She wrapped her arm around me, and this time, I leaned into her touch. In her presence, it felt like I was in the sun — warm and comforted.

We headed toward the exit with my bags when Kenya stopped with a funny look on her face.

"Uh oh, hold this," she said, pushing the bags into my hands and clutching her stomach. "I think that second Starbucks coffee is making a surprise reappearance." She dashed off to the bathroom, and I didn't know if I should be embarrassed or concerned.

I found a cozy nook in the store and waited for Kenya to come out. I picked out one of my books and started flipping through the pages. I started to imagine myself on my own journey exploring a new world, but this time, I wasn't doing it alone. I smiled when I pictured all the places my sister and I could go. Vegas. Greece. Spain. The possibilities were endless. I was deep in my story when I heard Kenya calling for me. She was near the cashier's station looking for me. I stood up and raised my hand.

I called back to her and waved until she saw me. She waved back, her oversized gold bracelet shining beneath the lights. She smiled and I did the same.

Then. A loud boom.

I almost fell to my knees but steadied myself on a shelf nearby.

After a stunned silence, panicked screams filled the air. The low rumble of falling books thundered. Black smoke flooded in, and a painful, dry cough ravaged my body as it tried to expel bits of paper and dust.

Another boom.

The entire building rocked as if it had been punched on all sides. Confusion flashed across everyone's faces before their expressions turned to terror. It wasn't long before people came rushing past me, knocking me into the bookcase, sprawling me on the floor. Blood pounded in my ears, and I found myself in a daze. When I finally stood up again, my eyes darted around. Bursts of orange flames lit up the store's corners, and bodies lay prone on the ground. My shirt clung to me from the sweat, but ice was running through me. Something rattled beside me, and I realized the sounds came from the bags in my hands. I was shaking. And now, I couldn't move. My feet were melded into the ground.

"Nettie!" Kenya called.

I locked eyes with her, and her expression was frantic. She was running toward me, trying to push past the crowd running to the exit. "Nettie, move!" Her arms reached for me over the wall of people that kept us apart. I wanted to go to her, but I couldn't. More smoke filled the room, and I could smell something burning. Paper, people, maybe both, I wasn't sure, but I knew I had to get out of there. I knew I had to get to Kenya. I screamed at my body with everything inside me, *MOVE!* My foot lifted.

A second explosion went off toward the front of the store, and the last thing I remember seeing was Kenya, her eyes wide open, looking at me, screaming something, but I couldn't hear her voice above the chaos. Her lips moved again, and it was like time slowed down, so I could read what her lips were saying.

"I'll come for you."

Then, she was gone.

Thrown across the room, I collided with a wall or bookcase. I couldn't tell which it was, but on impact, something cracked inside me. I was on the ground and could only hear glimpses of what was happening around me. More people running and screaming, shelves and walls crumbling. The entire second floor collapsed, and I'm sure I saw people falling. Blood ran into my eyes, causing my vision to go blurry. I wanted to move, but the pain was so intense I couldn't feel what parts of me were still there. It was too much. I had to get to Kenya.

I tried crawling to where I last saw her, but the room was spinning, so I couldn't tell if I had moved. Everything around me was growing darker. My pain was growing deeper, but the sounds around me were fading. I tried to wipe some of the blood from my eyes before my sight was completely gone. I looked for her. My sister. My mouth opened to call out her name, but by then, I couldn't hear a thing. Everything was drifting away from me. The bookstore. My sister. Myself. I used all my might to scream, but I don't know if anything came out. Then, it was black.

✳ ✳ ✳

When I woke up, it was like lightning struck me. Every inch of my skin pulsated with the pain of a thousand needles. Once the ringing in my ears settled down, I could tune into the noise around me. It was quieter than it was before. No screaming, falling, or exploding. I only heard the low moans of people who were buried around me. There was rubble on the floor, and the place had gone dark except for the areas where the flames blazed hungrily. The fire was drawing near me. I tried to move my body but screamed out in pain. My brain was foggy. One moment, I was standing there looking at Kenya, the next everything was gone. I tried to turn my head to check my surroundings, but the pain was indescribable.

Who would do something like this?

I picked up a faint noise, and I listened hard to it. Sirens.

Thank God help was on the way. I reached my hand out and attempted to drag myself once more. It felt like every muscle was tearing inside me as I dragged myself along, but I knew I had to keep going. I had to find my sister.

The path toward the entrance was non-existent. Chunks of the building had collapsed, and I had to force myself over fallen bookcases, broken glass, and other unknowable debris. There was too much wind, which meant the front of the store was gone. I could feel a breeze from the outside, but it didn't soothe me.

I bit my lip as I pulled myself over more debris, ignoring my pain. My hands were bloodied, and I was too afraid to look back at my legs because I could feel nothing there. I kept calling out Kenya's name, fighting through the thick smoke that coated my throat. All around me, pages were burning in the store. Paper fragments floated down gently and landed on the ground with one last flash of orange before going out completely; entire stories turned to ash. I called for Kenya again.

"Anyone in there?" A man's voice called out, and I could hear glass breaking and something moving. I started to yell back but sucked in a mouthful of smoke that sent me into a coughing fit. When I finally stopped, more blood was on my hands. I wiped it on the floor in front of me and tried again.

"I'm here!" I yelled back to him. "My sister needs help."

There was a flurry of movement and voices that came from outside. I could hear something mechanical moving debris away. I wanted to keep crawling and searching for Kenya, but I was so exhausted that I was fighting to keep myself awake. Sweat and dust covered my skin, and there was a sharp, acidic taste in my mouth.

I'll come for you. Kenya's last words replayed in my head, and when I pictured her with that terrified look, I was fueled by adrenaline. We both had to get out of there. I dug my bloodied nails into a nearby piece of wood and pulled myself forward again. Everything had been so destroyed it was all unrecognizable, but when I saw the edge of the cashier station, I knew I was close.

I pushed myself forward until I found a small clearing near an aisle. The cashier's station was in full view, and my heart went into overdrive. I inched closer and searched the ground where I last saw her. I called for her but still heard nothing. I was about to round the corner of the cashier's desk when I saw something shine in the corner of my eye. I reached for it and almost dropped it once I realized what I was holding. Kenya's golden charm bracelet.

A horrible cry escaped me. I didn't want to think about what it could mean. I closed the jewelry in my fist and kept going. There was no way I would accept that my sister was gone. My body spasmed from the pain, making it impossible to move. I had no choice but to stop. Frustration surged in me, and I banged my fist into something nearby. The structure creaked, then rumbled, until it fell on top of me.

✳ ✳ ✳

"Can you hear me, Ma'am?"

The voice sounded distant. I cracked my eyes open and was stung by the brightness of the object in front of me. "If you can hear me, follow the light with your eyes." The bright flash darted left and right. I followed. The light clicked off, and the man disappeared off to the side. My body was stiff and sore, but it didn't feel like it was on a hard floor anymore. Instead, it swayed back and forth like I was strapped into something.

"Where am I?" My voice sounded hoarse, and the question came out scratched.

A woman with orange hair leaned forward and gave me a soft smile. "You're in an ambulance." Then her expression changed to a frown as she asked, "Do you remember what happened?"

I tried to look around me, but my neck was locked into something holding it in place.

"My sister," I said. The woman looked confused and leaned closer to hear me better. "My sister," I repeated. "Kenya."

She leaned back with worried eyes and glanced at the other EMT. She placed her hand on my arm. "I'm sorry. I don't know where your sister is, but there's help looking for her now." The woman looked at me with wet eyes, and I wondered if she could feel my pain.

Tears welled up in my eyes, and my entire body shook. The woman tightened her grip on me and gently told me to calm down. She said I had severe injuries and needed to be careful with my movement. But what did that all matter if my sister was gone? The devastation of knowing that my world was somewhere in that store and there was nothing I could do about it was too overwhelming.

The woman grabbed a tissue and dabbed at my eyes. "We'll find her," she said. "Just don't give up yet." She sat back and began to dig into something nearby. She pulled out a plastic bag that had an object in it. "Here, we found you holding this when we brought you in."

She placed Kenya's bracelet in my hand. It was cool to the touch. It looked like someone tried to clean the dust off, but it was still in good condition. Some of the charms were missing, but the most important one was still there. I rubbed my thumb against the hanging "K" as tears slipped down my face.

When I first saw the bracelet in the jewelry store, I had just turned twelve. I was scrambling to figure out what to get Kenya for her birthday, but when I saw it, I knew I had found her the perfect gift. When she put it on for the first time, she kept raising her wrist up to the sky to watch how the sun reflected on it. Every time I saw her after that, she always had it on.

I asked the EMT for help fastening the bracelet around my wrist. She gently latched it with the clasp. From the back window, I could see that the sun was starting to set, and only a few rays remained. I raised my arm to the light and the gold chain sparkled like it used to on her.

TROUBLE HELPING

J.P. HIGGINS

Just after dawn, I was in a rear-facing seat on the B Line southbound out of the valley. The car was packed with the earliest of the rush-hour crowd: maintenance men, cleaning ladies, nannies, and the like. I was looking for trouble.

Five rows back, a tired man sat facing me. His tiny eyes flickered and searched, then closed under frowning bushy white eyebrows. His mouth hung open and slack as he panted. Thick pink folds of his neck disappeared into the grimy collar of a worn-to-translucent short-sleeved shirt. On his head was a sweat-stained green ball cap, its brim flipped up like a challenge or a joke. His green cotton pants matched his cap. *Maybe a janitor, or a mechanic.*

Across the aisle from this man, a small girl whined and wriggled to be loose of her mother's grip. The man opened his eyes and turned only his wide eyeballs toward her. His blank face intrigued me: Was he irritated? Saddened? Remembering? He looked away, into space, then his chin dropped to his chest; he closed his eyes and pretended to sleep.

At the Universal Studios stop, his eyes popped open, flitted to the window, narrowed, and considered the comings and goings on the platform. He didn't move, and I couldn't read his emotions, but he was struggling to hide his discomfort.

The train started up, and his eyes closed again.

A young woman who'd just boarded placed her index finger gently on his shoulder, wanting the window seat beside him. He swung his legs into the aisle and admitted her without a word or a look. She sat and began to read a book. He moved his legs back, sighed, and shut his tiny eyes once more.

At the Hollywood/Highland stop, he woke, rose, and shuffled up the aisle, revealing tired, tightly laced athletic shoes. A hard, brown eyeglasses case strained his shirt pocket, and the fabric across his prominent belly was taut.

At the car door, he stopped and rested, gripping the chrome pole with thick and calloused fingers. Faded wings tattooed his forearm. As he waited, rocked by the braking train, his eyes met mine. The doors opened; he walked out.

I followed him.

I'm not a criminal or a stalker or any kind of a nut, but I could see I had work to do.

He climbed the stairs using the handrail. In the natural light at street level, he looked younger, though he moved with a sluggish stiffness.

He walked to a trash can, placed both his hands on its edge, leaned over, and vomited without losing his cap.

He stood erect and wiped his face, glanced at his wet hand, and wiped it on his shirt back. He looked at me. "Go away," he said.

He took a longer look at me, then turned away saying, "Don't want any!"

I followed from a distance as he shuffled west on Hollywood Boulevard and turned into the alley mid-block. Down the alley, he joined a small group standing at a chain-link gate.

When I was a child, my house burned down and we had to move to a smaller, older house. Years later, after a college party, I found myself at dawn, drunk, on that same sidewalk where our old house had been. There was a new, different house on it, but our tree fort was still in the tree out back. All the house windows were dark. From the front porch, a lantern fixture with a yellow bulb cast long shadows around the two bicycles lying on the front path. That yellow light made the green grass look like puke.

He waved to the group. There were handshakes, milling, muttering, some smiles. Soon the gate opened and they all entered and walked to the building's back door. A handwritten sign on the chain-link gate read, "Open Call 9 a.m." The sign over the building's door said, "James Doolittle Theater."

I slipped in a moment later.

Inside a tiled hallway, a young girl sat behind a folding table. She pointed to loose papers on the table. I picked up a few sheets. It was all dialogue. Nine men and three women sat in the hallway on folding chairs. The girl said to me, "Sign in. Take a seat. We'll call you."

On the first night I did Oklahoma! in high school, I forgot the lyrics in the middle of the love-song duet. The orchestra vamped through the chorus and verse without me. The girl singing with me tried to prompt me with whispers, but my mind stayed blank. The faces of the people in the first row twisted in sympathy, their heads rocking with the rhythm in a silent effort to reach me telepathically. I stood frozen.

Over the heroine's head I saw the faculty drama coach in the wings, eyes wide, a script in one hand and his other hand pumping in time with the music. He barked, "Sweetheart! They're suspecting things!"

I ran off stage, furious with myself, furious with the coach for mocking me. Much later, I realized he'd barked the song lyrics I'd forgotten.

Without speaking, I left the hallway, went uphill, and waited at the bus shelter on Hollywood.

In an hour, the old man emerged and walked my way. "Leave me alone," he said, shuffling.

"I want to help."

"I don't know you."

"You have trouble." I walked beside him.

"Get the hell away from me."

"I can help."

A young boy stood on the back of the empty bus bench, arms flailing, trying to balance like he was on a tightrope.

A woman, his mother, beside the bench said, "You be careful, Jocko!"

The old man stopped and grimaced. "Control that kid!" he shouted at the woman. "He's gonna kill himself!"

"Don't pay him any attention, Jocko," the woman said. She moved to stand between her boy and the old man. "Get away, old man!"

I stepped in closer and said, "I can help."

"Mind your own business," the old man shouted. He got so agitated as I approached that he stumbled off the curb and fell into the gutter in front of the bus bench. I bent to him, offering my hand.

After the U.S. Air Force, I used my savings as a down payment on a Wienerschnitzel franchise. They trained me in Ocala, Florida, for three weeks, then I took over a store in Flint, Michigan. (I loved that their corporate slang for the hotdog place was "the store." Made me feel like a merchant, like I had risen above what my grandmother called "my station in life.")

I owned the store four years; a worse four years than my Air Force hitch. The store's previous owner had been a white supremacist who'd deliberately poisoned some of his Black customers; he was ratted out by one of the dishwashers and jailed. He'd been a redhead, and when I showed up — another carrot top — the neighborhood thought I was a relative, boycotted me, and I never broke even. Lost everything.

Jocko had climbed off the bus bench. When the old man had fallen into the street, Jocko and his mother moved closer to him, silent and curious.

The man's tiny eyes narrowed, and he turned away from me, flinching in fear.

"I was an actor too," I said.

His eyes widened in surprise and suspicion, then softened like a helpless aged leprechaun caught with his gold exposed, hoping against fear.

"Get me up," he ordered.

The skin of his hand was rough, and he was heavier than I'd guessed.

As I got the old man to the bench, the woman pulled the boy closer to her.

"You're an awful mother," shouted the old man, waving his arm as if swatting at a swarm of gnats.

"My ass!" she shouted back.

Is that the best she can do? I thought, disappointed. I'd learned a thing or two about insults at Der Wienerschnitzel.

Now sitting, the old man straightened his shirt and dusted off his pants as best he could reach them over his belly.

"Who are you?" he said to me, still suspicious.

The TV announcer spoke with that false enthusiasm they all have. "Today's winner is Michael Biedelman! From Van Nuys, Californay-yah-ah-AH!"

I've watched my tape ten dozen times (at least). Can't get over the goofy look in my eyes. They put a lot of makeup on me, and I look like a cardboard cutout of myself, like in my high school Oklahoma! pictures. But the whole time on that TV show I felt nervous and awkward. I slouched too much and looked ordinary.

"Tell us, Michael," said the announcer. "What are you going to do now that you've won sixteen million dollars in the lottery?"

He wasn't even looking at me. He was twitching and looking over my shoulder at something way out of the camera frame.

"Maybe I'll help some people?" I mumbled. "I don't know, really. Stay out of trouble, I hope."

"He's going to help people stay out of trouble!" shouted the announcer as he put his hand on my shoulder and turned toward the camera. "Isn't that fantastic, folks?"

"Who am I?" I said to the old man. "I'm the kid you knew back in school who was always in trouble, always had to sit in front of the teacher, or always put in the corner, or sent to the principal's office. I'm that guy. But I've grown up and don't want to be that guy anymore. I want to help people. I want to be the opposite of a troublemaker. So, I've got a question for you."

The old man flinched a bit; his brows lifted and his eyes widened.

"Will you let me help you?"

He pursed his lips and looked down. "No. I don't want your help."

"Okay," I nodded. I turned to the young mother. "How about you? Need help?" She held her son a bit tighter and shook her head.

Maybe it's just something about L.A., but this is what happens to me. Not every time, but more often than you would think.

THE MAKEUP LESSON

SARAH HAUFRECT

I remember how I lifted my window shade as the plane's wheels hit the blacktop, squinting at the bright shock of light coming over the mountains beyond Burbank. I remember the crinkling sound of the crumpled, half-eaten packet of mini pretzels in my lap as I rummaged in my carry-on for sunglasses while taxiing to the gate, how I considered finishing the pretzels off, but hesitated, desperately missing the honey-roasted peanuts the airline used to serve. They had been the perfect snack: salty and fatty and sweet and never enough to ruin a meal. After savoring each individual peanut, I'd lick my index finger and press it into the back corner of the empty bag like a FunDip, dredging up the last crystals of honeyed salt and sucking on my finger like I'd pricked it. I could easily buy a whole canister of the same nuts at the market, but it wasn't the same. I wanted the ritual as much as I wanted the taste. It's funny the things we remember.

I heard the ding of the seatbelt sign turning off, cracking knuckles, cell phone alerts, and the synchronous rumble of weight shifting from seated to standing. A few rows back, a baby started to fuss in an indecisive fashion, and the mother made a verbal show of trying to soothe the half-cries. But when the sun pried through the cabin door, the baby started to wail at the cruelty of light. *Get used to it, kid*, I thought. No matter how many times I'd ridden this fifty-five-minute arc across the sky from foggy SFO, the brightness never ceased to unnerve me.

On this particular trip, I had several reasons to be more unsettled: I hadn't seen my mother in years, I hadn't told my father I'd be seeing her before heading to his house, and I hadn't told my fiancé either. "A quick trip home," was what I'd told them both. A slippery lie of omission for sure, but at least a kind one, the way I saw it. *First, do no harm.* That was going to be the mandate of my professional life, the oath to which I would swear. At the time, I justified this act as good practice.

We disembarked down the shaky metal stairway, filing out in ragged lines from the front and back of the plane. I stepped onto the tarmac and faced the scraggly mountains, patchy and uneven, like my dad's ill-fated attempts to grow a beard. The black surface below my feet jittered and waved with engine exhaust. I was home.

At the car-rental lot, I handed the paperwork over to the attendant at the exit kiosk, who reviewed the documents and my driver's license while I fumbled with the A/C controls on the dash, then used my knee to hold the steering wheel steady as I took off my sweater. I stared at the steel claws poking out of the ground, then read the warning, "Do Not Backup. Severe Tire Damage." The point of no return.

"Need directions?" the attendant asked, handing the materials back.

"Thanks. But I'm all set."

I pulled out of the lot, the car tires trundling over the steel teeth, and took solace in the thought of returning to Jake's place — no, to *our place* — in a few days. Change, even good change, was uncomfortable. The apartment was fine, though. Nicer than some of the places I'd lived with my dad growing up, I'd told Jake, and meant it. That's when Jake asked me to count all the houses I'd lived in before we met. We sat on his couch with coffee mugs filled to the brim with red Gatorade, the only thing I liked to drink lately, and I listed them. The grand total was seven; none of them more than a dozen miles apart but each with a new name and ZIP code. Sherman Oaks, Tarzana, Toluca Lake, Sunland, Encino, Van Nuys, and Universal City. Jake marveled at the names like they were exotic destinations rather than quiet suburbs. He had grown up in Oakland in the same house his parents lived in now, a short drive from the family business, which was a dry cleaner near the Ashby BART station. But Jake and I were alike in the way our parents urged us to find our own professional paths. My dad wanted me to have absolutely nothing to do with the entertainment industry, and neither did I.

I could have taken the freeway but opted for surface streets, noting what had changed and what had stayed the same as I passed from Burbank to Valley Village to Studio City. The San Fernando Valley was being nipped and tucked and smoothed over, just like many of its residents. Chic apartment complexes with names like The Moderno or Gallery Lofts surrounded the metro station in NoHo, displacing the small theaters and family-run restaurants from my childhood. There was always at least one new coffee house, yoga studio, or smoothie bar with every visit home, but I took comfort in the steadfast strip mall at Woodman and Moorpark where my beloved donut shop remained firmly entrenched, with the same sign in the window for a small free coffee with every donut. I planned to ask my dad if we could stop by the next morning, even if the coffee had to be decaf for me.

Twenty minutes and two new yoga studios later, the little silver rental and I spiraled up Lookout Mountain Road, its slow coil of incline feeling steeper than I remembered. I fluffed the top of my dress with one hand and wished I'd put on more deodorant. Over the years, I'd tried everything short of Botox injections to quell the dark, sticky patches of anxiety sweat from spreading under my arms and between my thighs, but it was no use. And I wasn't willing to consider an injectable toxin now that my body was a safe house, a temporary haven for the microscopic guests inside my ovaries. In this outfit — a dress that used to fit, but was easily a size too small now, strappy platform heels, shiny gratuitous belt — I felt uncomfortable inside my own skin, but I had dressed for my intended audience, and Jake had been too groggy with sleep when I'd kissed him goodbye to even notice the uncharacteristic nature of this ensemble. I could blame the hormones for the weight gain, the mandated rest, and the shots, but I'd been careless, and I knew it, letting the hours of studying for my boards give way to a steady stream of extra calories. The larger breasts were quite the novelty, though, and Jake certainly didn't mind, but he still retained mixed feelings that the eggs growing in my ovaries would pay for the wedding, the honeymoon, for things we couldn't afford otherwise. My feelings on the subject were clear: finding solutions gave me satisfaction, and donating my eggs was a solution.

I pulled into a parking spot close to her house, but not too close. The tall oak branches pressed in against the glass of the passenger side and made a sound against the windshield like sandpaper. I took a deep breath and picked up my purse. Halfway to the house, it became clear that I'd parked farther than I'd thought, or maybe walking in heels made the distance feel longer. Or maybe my body was feeling the weight of its new passengers. I was hungry and cranky; I wanted this to be over and it hadn't even started.

I made it to the call box, noted the shiny new security cameras. Privacy and security were prized possessions here. I pressed the buzzer on the number pad for guests. The sound reminded me of the old dial-up noise before wireless internet. After a moment, its fuzzy whir cut out and there was only silence on the other end. It was time to announce myself.

"Hi. It's me," I said, and then felt compelled to add, "it's Beth," though the need to say my name felt a little like an insult to both of us.

There was a pause, a click, and then a rumble. The gate began its slow retreat behind the wall. I walked up the incline towards the house and up the steps, then pressed the doorbell. I smoothed out the front of my sandy hair. Most would say it was blonde, but not here. At best, my hair was tawny, and in the heat, my bangs frizzed with anxiety. I looked at the wrought iron chandelier hanging above me, looming as monstrous as ever. If a Northridge-level earthquake were to hit, the whole thing would come down and crush me in one fatal blow. Being at this particular doorstep put me in the mood to contemplate natural disasters.

The door opened. She wore sunglasses and had her hair pulled so high up on her head that her ponytail flared in all directions like a platinum feather duster. She pulled the plastic white-rimmed lenses down towards the tip of her tiny nose and the painted lines of her eyebrows appeared. From there, she flipped the glasses up to rest on her head. I took a good look at her face in the same way I surveyed the city, looking for the features that had and hadn't changed. It had been a long time.

"Hi Mom."

✳ ✳ ✳

When I'd first brought up egg donation to Jake, we were stuffing our faces with roasted garlic spread at a touristy spot in Little Italy anxiously awaiting our main course. We'd taken BART into the city for Valentine's Day in order to, in Jake's words, cliché it up, for our first post-engagement date.

"Do you know how much my unfertilized eggs are worth on the open market?" I said.

"This is your idea of romantic dinner conversation?"

I situated the lit candle on the table for an Instagram story with us clinking our glasses.

"Up to $50,000."

Jake almost spit out his wine.

"If I'm just a normal donor and do it six times, it's about 12K a pop," I explained. "But since I'm young and college educated with no big scary diseases in the family, I might qualify as a premium donor."

Jake swirled the Chianti in his wine glass and mulled this information over. "Do I make that much for jacking off into a cup and giving it to a sperm bank?"

"No, sperm donation's more like an ongoing thing, like a subscription or gym membership for your penis. Maybe $150 per time, or $1,000 a month or something."

The waiter arrived with the entrees, so we silenced our talk of body parts and body fluids and turned our attention to the celebratory feast. We swirled spaghetti on spoons and covered our napkins with splotches of marinara. We didn't save room for dessert, but we ordered it anyway. Full and tired, sitting extra close on the empty subway car heading back on the Richmond line, Jake had looked at our shared reflection in the window and said, "I bet you'd be a premium donor."

* * *

My mother led me through the entryway and down the steps into her sitting room. The carpeting was the same: a muted pink the color of raw chicken.

"Can I get you anything?" my mother asked, looking disoriented in her own home. "I was so surprised to get your call last week." She'd never known what to do with me and still didn't. She shifted the weight of her oblong torso, teetering about in wooden platform mules.

I almost ignored her question, as I was too busy browsing the room and comparing it to images from the last time while she was arranging things that appeared over arranged to begin with, compulsively trying to keep her hands busy with the vases and knockoff Lladro figurines in erotic shapes and sexualized positions. The tan cylindrical vase covered in dozens of breasts was situated as it had been years before, by the side of the couch, holding thin stalks of fabricated Pussywillow.

"I'm good for now, thanks," I said. "It was a last-minute trip, and there was a sale on Southwest."

She propped herself up against the voluminous cushions lining the white leather couch. I sat facing her on a zebra patterned swivel chair.

"How've you been, Mom?"

"Me? Oh, my life is full of blessings," she said. "I've been getting more work, and Todd's been away on another film." She opened up the drawer on the table next to her and pulled out a bottle of pearlescent nail polish. "Do you mind? One of them chipped right before you got here."

"How is Todd?" I asked, hoping the pleasantry would cover the bad taste his name left in my mouth.

"One of his films won an award recently." She shook the polish, her top half shaking like gelatin, and opened up the top, dabbed the tiny brush on her nail.

"That's great," I offered, "about the award." Todd had to pay for this ridiculous house somehow.

"Best Sex Comedy," she said, fanning the polish and smiling absently, looking everywhere but into my eyes. Perhaps it was because our eyes were one of the few genetic traits we shared, and that she couldn't alter. "Lemme tell ya, it was a hoot."

I sat in that moment quietly, not knowing how to respond. Looking at my mother felt like looking into a funhouse mirror. I wondered if she felt the same way looking at me.

"So, you're still acting, then?" I tried not to sound overly surprised, but I couldn't help but wonder.

"Me? No, not really acting, only special appearances. Conventions, you know. I'm so past my prime, but Todd tells me I'm like a fine wine; I just get better with age."

"You look beautiful, Mom."

"Aww, shucks," she said with content, blowing on her retouched fingernail. "And look at you! You look so . . ." She paused here and searched for her words. "So happy."

She leaned back and produced a sound like a tuning fork, a long high *Mmmmmmmm*. It was like her signature frequency, her nervous tick during pauses in conversations. It was almost like a homing device, getting shorter and shriller as she neared a sentient thought. I could handle the physical stuff all right, but the worst part was her voice. There was something about modifying her voice that still felt shocking. Shocking because, to my knowledge, she hadn't surgically changed it. Her voice was something she had to actively work to alter every time she spoke. That kind of commitment to her new self never ceased to confound me. I'd forgotten the sound of her real voice long ago. "And how about your father? Remarried?"

"No, not yet," I said. "A few girlfriends here and there, but …" I trailed off, thinking of the women that flitted in and out of his life like his leased cars, shiny and new for a couple years before he'd turn them back in for a new one with a cheaper monthly payment.

"I'm a tough act to follow," she said as somberly as her chipmunk tone could manage. "You know, Bethany —"

I braced for her to deliver the speech I'd heard all my life.

"I'm the first to admit that your father and I are not perfect. We made mistakes and we were not meant to be together. You understand though, right? I had to follow my dreams and it was really all for the best. He took very good care of you. Better than I ever could. And, well, Todd takes care of me."

"I know, Mom."

I didn't remind her that he'd taken care of us both. I'd seen the court documents. He'd paid alimony for years, but this wasn't the point of my visit. Her view of the past and my view of it didn't have to add up to truth.

"Speaking of getting married, Mom, I came to see you because I have some news. Jake and I are engaged."

Her mouth formed a weak smile. "But you're still a baby."

"I'm twenty-six."

"No, that can't be true?" She said like it was a question that had just now miraculously occurred to her. She'd married my father, a man fifteen years her senior, when she was twenty-one, but I didn't bring that up.

My mother looked down at my left hand, my ring finger, and a hint of confusion crossed her placid, wrinkle-free face before it turned to mild disappointment at the small pearl neatly set in ten-carat gold.

"He's a really good guy, an architect," I said. Although this was forward-leaning, aspirational language, he was certainly on track to be an architect. "And planning would be almost impossible if we waited longer, since I'll be finishing with my residency next year, while he's finishing grad school, so this is the right window."

"Always so practical," she said, shaking her ponytail. "You've got all those brains and book smarts from your grandmother, God rest her soul." She smoothed back her hair with her hands, brushed her fingers through her fine, pale tresses to keep them busy. "You know what, we should have champagne! Let me make us mimosas to celebrate."

I followed her into the kitchen, where the décor shifted to chrome and marble; counters and fixtures that were easy to clean and rarely used for cooking. Sterile. Regretfully, I was aware that Todd had a quote-unquote "successful" series of videos called *Brunch Babes* that made me try to touch as little as possible in this kitchen. I took a small sip of the spiked orange juice from its crystal flute and set it down, reasoning the alcohol would kill whatever germs I might ingest. We partook in the exercise of chitchat, exchanging information about the years when our lives had little intersection. I thought about my Facebook profile, plucking the past for notable updates to share with her, focusing only on the highlights. She poured herself a second mimosa while I sipped mine timidly, worried it might affect the eggs.

My mother displayed an impressive grasp of wedding-related knowledge for someone who'd eloped, divorced, and never technically remarried. Then again, it seemed that women were born with some genetic knowledge of marriage and its rituals, sort of like the inherited trauma I'd studied in one of my psych courses.

"You know, Beth," she said with some trepidation in her tone, "if you have a little more time, I was thinking, maybe I could give you a makeup lesson?"

I was wearing tinted sunscreen and a sweep of mascara. That was all I ever wore. Elaborate makeup had never been something that made me look better. It only made me look like I was wearing makeup and caused acne on my chin. I looked at my mother's eyes, pliant only at the corners. A makeup lesson: that was the thing that made her feel like an expert, the gift she wanted to give, was capable of giving.

"Sure," I said.

She made a high-pitched gasp that sounded like air squeaking out of an unsealed balloon. "Really? You mean it?"

"I mean it," I said.

∗　∗　∗

Jake and I had talked about having kids together in the abstract, aspirational way I talked about learning French or running a marathon, something that required long-term planning, commitment, and discipline. It was the same way I probably talked about wanting to be a doctor in elementary school. Now I was on that real journey and feeling ready, feeling like I'd put in the time and effort to earn the accomplishment. I thought of Jake's final remark about my anti-Müllerian hormone test, the one indicating my ideal candidacy as a donor, when I showed him my A-plus score. He'd said, "Look at you, acing a test and you didn't even have to study." Maybe if other people raised children that grew from my grade-A eggs, it would be okay if I eventually decided not to have any myself. I liked the idea of ushering babies into the world, not as a mother, but as a doctor. I didn't see my-self as a mother; I certainly hadn't seen myself in my own mother.

* * *

My mother led the way to the staircase, and we descended into the belly of her bizarre residence. This house wasn't like the Hollywood hillside homes off Mulholland; those luxurious mansions seen from the main road poking out of the mountains on stilts. Conversely, this home was three floors deep with the entrance on the top level, its staircase spiraling down to the lower two floors tucked deep into the canyon and overlooking a gully of velvety foliage. The middle floor opened up into a large den with too many places to lie down, plus a giant bar along the far wall that looked out on dense greenery along the side of the house. I was shocked to see a girl, perhaps my age, perhaps younger, compressed in the far corner, luxuriating with a beauty magazine obscuring her face. She wore a cotton robe that displayed two long legs twisted like rope, her hair covered by a mess of towel. The vent in the nearby bathroom was still going.

"Up early, are we?" my mother said. The girl lowered the magazine and gave my mother a view of her skinny middle finger. I waited for my mother to offer up an introduction to the girl, but none came. Instead, I smiled and waved half-heartedly as we passed her.

We pressed onward, down the stairs to the master bedroom, with its sprawling California king center stage on the dark hardwood floor. A rumpled leopard print comforter spilled down off the unmade bed exposing white silk sheets, so shimmery they looked wet.

"Who was that?" I asked.

"Todd's stepdaughter, well *ex*-stepdaughter, what do you call that? Anyhoo, she had trouble in school. Authority issues or something. Doesn't play well with others, but Todd gave her some other options. She's perfect as a cam girl, and so much safer, can make her own hours," she said. "I think she's warming up to me."

"Must be a really good income," I said, as long as Todd wasn't taking it all. I made a note to do an incognito search on my phone for the amount of money girls made to take their clothes off in front of a webcam for anonymous viewers across the distant, sterile internet. Then I thought about how many fluids and hands and instruments had already, and would continue to, penetrate me to extract the donor eggs from my body.

* * *

What my mother did for a living was the one secret I kept from the man I was going to marry. Most of the time, I didn't even feel guilty about it. It was an odd thing to consider the genuine possibility that Jake had at some point in his life seen my mother naked. I decided to save him from having to consider this question himself.

* * *

We reached the master bathroom, where the bulbs on the side of the mirror reached up to the ceiling and haloed the space in a dim yellow glow that smoothed out imperfections of the face and body with soft, pleasing light. My mother flicked the overhead light on with one of her fingernails and everything came into sharper focus. I surveyed the counter spilling over with an arsenal of products to fight the process of aging in the natural world. My mother hummed and flitted about like a nesting bird until there were a dozen different containers of all shapes and sizes in front of us.

"You've always had your father's bone structure," she said, as one of her long nails softly grazed my cheek. "Have you heard of facial contouring? You can actually change the shape of your face with a brush and the right shadows." She took out a thick bottle of foundation and shook it. Her breasts wobbled at a different rate than her rest of her torso. She nabbed a foundation applicator pad from a glass container, layered it with thick facial paint, and started lacquering my face.

"Chin up," she requested, pressing the foam applicator against my jawbone. "This is a great base layer. I'm so glad you have my coloring." She worked rapidly, humming all the while. Before I knew it, my face was one solid, impenetrable color. Not a single freckle to be seen.

"Tabula rasa," I said.

"Tabula whatah?"

"Sorry, it means blank slate in Latin. I look like a bare canvas."

"So much like your nana," she repeated. "Shame you never got to meet her. Mommy loved Scrabble, did the crossword every Sunday. When she was a girl, they put her in a hospital for six weeks, you know. Some sort of German diet cure. She lost twenty-five pounds, and then they sent her home. Good practice for the war, I guess."

Tales of Nana. I couldn't escape them. I honestly wished I could have met her. She went to medical school and was in residency in Hamburg when the war broke out. She started faking medical records for the Jewish patients, saying they were much sicker than they actually were, too sick to leave the hospital or infectious. And once the soldiers had left, she would get them discharged. That's the part of the story I like; that she was crafty and smart, that she figured out how to take the worst situation and do something heroic. But that's not the end of the story.

"Do you remember what she always told me?" she asked.

She would never let me forget. My mother paused.

I remember the pause. *She's not going to say it. She wants me to say it, to prove I remember her favorite part of the story.*

"The reason the doctors listened to her, the reason the Nazi soldiers believed her, the reason she could get away with things, wasn't because she was clever; it was because she was pretty. She said that being pretty is what saved her life."

A photo of my grandmother was set at an angle on the vanity counter in an ornate gold frame. It was taken after she'd made it to Texas, remarrying after her first husband was lost to her. She never practiced medicine again. In that image, her bouffant hairstyle was majestic, like the Eiffel Tower lit up at night. No level of photographic weathering could dim the shocking blue of her eyes. I was probably in my mother's womb at the time the photo was taken, maybe a few months shy of the car accident.

My mother and I regarded the photo in its frame, the reflection of all three of us in the mirror, sharing one dimension.

"Exactly," she said.

Later on, as my mother was walking me to the door, on what seemed like a whim, she insisted we take a picture together, giving Todd's ex-stepdaughter her cellphone to take it. Then, my mother asked for my phone, not hers, to take a closeup of my face, to reproduce the look for my wedding day, in case she couldn't make it. When I left, she kissed the air above my cheek, closed the door, and sent me back into my life.

As I waited for the gate to open, I looked at the photo of my face, with all the color and drama my mother had layered upon it. I let my gaze move below my phone screen and down to my body. I rested a hand on my abdomen and said a little prayer for all the lives inside me that I would never know.

* * *

Months later, I sent my mother an invitation to the wedding. Even though I didn't expect her to attend, I figured she'd at least respond, but I never heard anything back. I called to check if she received the invite and left her a message, which she did not return, and that seemed like enough of an answer.

For the wedding, I could have hired a professional makeup artist; instead, I asked for a little privacy to get ready, took out my phone, and found the photo, not to reproduce it faithfully, but to guide my hand and still look like myself. At various points throughout the ceremony, I glanced around the room scanning all the guests. *Maybe she might show up unannounced?* Part of me wanted her there, and part of me feared the uncertainty her presence would create at an event where I'd planned every last thing. Regardless, I could not find her face in the crowd.

* * *

I didn't know that visit would be the last time I would see her until recently. I was watching the *In Memoriam* segment of the Oscars at a viewing party when her image and name passed across the screen, my entire body seized up with disbelief. I was glad Jake was not there because he would have noticed immediately and asked what was wrong. A call came through almost immediately from my father, who may have also been in a state of shock, but I silenced his call. Sitting on a couch, surrounded by a group made up in equal parts of friends and strangers, I shrunk into the cushions with my phone angled away from anyone else's view and typed her name into a search engine, something I'd avoided after doing it one too many times in my youth. It turned out that early in her career, before she'd ever met my father, she'd starred in several mainstream films as the young heroine. How did I never know this? At that age, her face looked just like mine.

After they announced the Best Picture winner, I excused myself and texted Jake that I was leaving the party and would be home soon. I was glad to have the train ride to myself, to summon up what I could remember of that day so many years ago. I took out my phone and scrolled until I found the picture. Since I never told anyone that I saw her, and since she never sent me the picture of us together, my only evidence of seeing her that day was this picture of my face in full makeup, and I was grateful I had kept it. For the rest of the train ride home, I stared out the dark window at my own reflection.

SOUL-SEARCHING IN TOPANGA CANYON

LAURA MCGHEE

When I moved to L.A., this was my policy: if someone invited me out somewhere, and I didn't think that attending the occasion would result in my death, then I was going to accept. And that is how I ended up at a séance in Topanga Canyon.

I had arrived eight months earlier, without enough savings, without a compelling enough demo reel, and without nearly enough industry contacts. My plan was to network my way into opportunities, so I immersed myself in L.A.'s social scene. A typical week saw me hiking past the Hollywood Sign, sipping a martini at Musso & Frank, and meandering through The Grove. But like so many other transplants, my income didn't stretch as far as I thought it would. So, my outings quickly devolved into anything that was gratuite — especially if it involved food. Art gallery openings, Shabbat gatherings, and Oscar parties were my mainstays. Nevertheless, I calculated that I could ostensibly hang in there for about three more months before I was going to have to head home with my tail between my legs … home being a tiny town in Iowa that could only recently boast of the presence of an Arby's. Since nearly everybody in my life had discouraged me from making this move in the first place, this was not a prospect that appealed to me. And would likely appeal to me even less in three months, when it would be February in the Midwest but still July in Los Angeles.

So, my neighbor, Lorna, could not have timed her invitation better. Lorna was a party planner — excuse me, an event organizer — whom I had been mercilessly nagging to take me along to any or all of her gigs, in the hope of making a connection. So far, she had stonewalled me, but when I ran into her at the mailboxes, she actually initiated the offer.

"One of my clients is hosting a salon this Wednesday night. It sounds like it's going to be really French. They're serving hors d'oeuvres. Are you avail?"

Free food. Très bien.

"That sounds great! Would you mind driving? My car's in the shop."

I couldn't afford gas.

Lorna agreed and several evenings later, we crawled our way up the PCH — Pacific Coast Highway — to South Topanga Canyon Boulevard. Driving anywhere in Los Angeles County was a super-fun game of punctuality roulette. A fourteen-minute journey could take fourteen minutes, forty minutes, or four hours, depending on traffic. It could also take no time at all; if the area you were traveling to was on fire, you would simply be unable to get there, period. The canyons were particularly challenging, because generally, there was only one way in and one way out.

"That's why I'd never buy here," Lorna remarked as we chatted in the gridlock.

"Oh, me too!" I declared.

I had eight hundred dollars in my checking account. And it was already the last week of the month, which was always bad news for anyone not still living with their parents.

After somewhere between forty-five minutes and two hours (you learned to just ignore the construct of time in L.A. traffic), we pulled into an impossibly long and sinewy gravel driveway. The house that eventually revealed itself was a celebration of cedar shingles, imported cypress trees, and tastefully placed dreamcatchers. The chickens clucking away in their architecturally designed coop were clearly organic and free range. It was where you'd imagine hippies would live if they were rich.

"Whose place is this?" I finally asked. I'd been dying to know for days, but I wanted to stay classy.

"*****," Lorna whispered excitedly.

"Oh, I love *****!"

***** had starred on a popular TV series in the late seventies, which he had then parlayed into a series of romantic made-for-TV movies. The majority of them co-starred Kristy McNichol. But I hadn't seen him in anything for quite some time.

"He's a wildly successful artist now," Lorna said.

That explained it.

***** and his wife, $$$$$, a former swimsuit model and activist, met us at the front door. They were both effusively welcoming, and their hairless Persian cat only bit me once. Iago was given a time-out in the pantry; I was given a small tube of Arnica cream.

After a few more guests had congregated, we were given a tour, commencing way up in the "atelier." The attic was completely devoid of any furnishings or decoration, save for a wooden café chair, and an easel, which had a blank white canvas mounted on it. We all spewed witticisms on the theme of Marie Kondo while our host grinned conspiratorially by the doorway.

Then he flicked the light switch off, and the room was illuminated by phosphorescent paint. Every square inch was covered with incomprehensible swirls and symbols in multiple colors and styles. I had no idea that so many shades of pink and purple existed or that every single painting style — Gothic, Renaissance, Baroque, Expressionist, Impressionist, Abstract, and somehow, even Minimalist — could be represented in one work. It was chaotic … like Bob Ross on acid. I felt nauseated.

"This is absolutely stunning," I gushed.

***** beamed. "Glad you like it! I've got three more floors to show you!"

By the time we reached the living room, I was disoriented and soaked with sweat. I could barely choke down eight canapés and three glasses of Chablis. We were ushered to our seats, facing a makeshift stage, composed largely of yoga mats. I sank down shakily, grateful that this room was art-free. ***** ventured barefoot to centerstage.

"Ladies and gentlemen, we thank you so much for joining us this evening in our monthly salon. The goal of these evenings is to enlighten and expand our horizons. So, we ask that you keep an open mind to go along with your open heart. As Jean-Luc Godard once said, 'Life has no meaning the moment you lose the illusion of being eternal.'"

"That was Jean-Paul Sartre," I murmured to Lorna.

"Shh!"

And then the lights slowly dimmed in a way that made me wonder for a millisecond if I was having a stroke. When they came back up, HE was sitting in front of us with his hands on his knees. HE appeared to be a slightly built white man with blond-layered bangs, wearing a pair of relaxed-fit Levis, a black Gap t-shirt, and a pair of hi-tops.

A ripple of excitement ran through the audience. There was even a smattering of applause from a few people. I could only imagine the ovation HE would have received if he'd gone all out and worn socks.

HE explained to us that HE was a channeler of spirits. HE never knew who was going to arrive, if anyone, to use his body as a conduit. In fact, HE couldn't guarantee that anything would happen that evening, but HE would try his best. Of course, it was beyond his control; ultimately it was up to the spirits.

Based on his attire, I was certain HE was about to channel someone from a regional improv troupe. But as I was thinking about what I would shout out when HE asked for a suggestion of an occupation, HE touched his forefingers to his thumbs, and his eyes rolled back in his head. HE flopped forward in his chair and stayed that way for an uncomfortable amount of time. A gasp of discomfort rippled through the audience. $$$$$ made an attempt to reach the stage but ***** held her back.

"Give him some room!" ***** exclaimed.

I really wanted another Chablis.

Then HE abruptly raised his head. His posture had changed. HE was rigid and coiled. His eyes were narrowed and angry. And his voice was different … kind of.

HE introduced himself as Chief Redfeather. HE told us that he was the chief of a tribe from the Pacific Northwest (nothing more specific than that) and that HE had died in a great battle in the eighteen hundreds against a warring tribe … again, no specifics. HE shared that he had many children, made a joke about his virility, and then yelled at a woman in the front row for not turning her cell phone off.

I turned to Lorna. "How does he know what a cell phone is?"

"Shh!"

Next, HE treated us to some bad mime by pulling something invisible out of his pocket and then chewing on it quite aggressively.

"Is that pemmican??" The cell phone woman had clearly regained her composure.

He grunted in response.

She turned and addressed the crowd. "I think it is!"

More applause.

I couldn't tell where the next question came from, but it was the perfect red-carpet query.

"What are you wearing?"

Another grunt.

"A headdress?"

A grunt and a nod.

"Moccasins?"

A barely perceptible smile.

"Um … a string of scalps?"

This time, HE stretched himself artistically by emitting a low chuckle, which evoked a squeal from the audience. HE waited for the room to settle before HE performed a native chant that sounded a lot like "MMMBop" by Hanson.

The tiniest of laughs escaped my lips. Really, the sound was so subtle it could have been attributed to seasonal allergies. But apparently not subtle enough.

"SHH!!!"

This time the shushing wasn't just Lorna's. Everywhere I looked, there were angry stares … even from the caterer. But the caterer might have been thinking about the eight canapés I snagged. And that's when I realized that everyone in that room, had bought into this lunatic's dog-and-pony show. Everyone except me.

I was completely alone.

After Chief Redfeather's indigenous liturgy, HE took more questions from the audience. And every single hand was up. The questions were completely unrelated to the life of native peoples in the early days of European settlement. Yet somehow, Chief Redfeather knew all the answers.

HE knew that the woman in the third row wearing hoop earrings should put her house on the market. HE knew that the elderly gentleman at the back should ignore his doctor's advice and go to Portugal. HE knew that three different audience members' spouses were cheating on them and that they should begin divorce proceedings post-haste. His advice was absolute and unwavering.

It was utterly immoral.

I felt a rage so visceral that it curled all the way up from my toes to my throat. I had to stop this. It wasn't right.

I raised my hand and jabbed the air. Lorna glared at me. I slowly lowered it.

Exactly one hour into this spiritual extravaganza, Chief Redfeather was suddenly seized by the same rolling back of the eyes and collapsing of the body. And then HE was gone. His earthly vessel then handed out business cards and told us that he booked private appointments for those who were brave enough to "delve deeper." Chief Redfeather was clearly a fan of both advertising *and* alliteration.

There was a line-up for the cards. Lorna stepped on my toe in her hurry to join it. Enroute, she comforted a woman who was openly sobbing.

"You know I've always suspected that she wasn't my birth mother!"

"I'm going to wait outside," I said.

Twenty minutes and two Luna bars later, Lorna joined me, and we drove off into the deep, dark night. I was expecting her to berate me for embarrassing her in front of her client and other potential clients, but she was surprisingly quiet. She finally opened her mouth as if to say something but closed it again. I decided it was best to clear the air. Besides, I was starting to suspect that Lorna wasn't as well connected as she had led me to believe.

"Something on your mind?" I asked.

Lorna pursed her lips. "It's just ... well ... I have to ask ... did that offend you, you know, as an atheist?"

I chortled. "Not exactly."

She tried again. "Well, did you find it problematic that a white man was portraying a Native American? Because cultural appropriation is a thing ... for real. Look at *Hamilton*, am I right?"

A series of small explosions went off in my head.

"What the hell are you talking about? No, I mean, of course, his performance was completely racist — that's a given. But it really offended me as an *actor*! That guy did zero preparation for that role. He had no origin story, no character details, and he couldn't even hold on to his accent. He kept slipping in and out of the physicality as well. It was total amateur hour back there!"

Lorna nodded slowly. "Wow, that's a really interesting take. I'm not an actor, so I didn't notice any of those things. So, you don't think Chief Redfeather is legit?"

I snorted. "He said he drove a Chevy Impala to the meeting of the tribal elders!!"

"And it was supposed to be the eighteen hundreds ... I get what you are saying." Lorna smiled.

"Thank you!!" I crossed my arms in arrogant vindication.

We stopped at the intersection leading back onto the PCH. Lorna dug a business card out of her phone case and placed it on the center console.

She chose her words carefully. "Yeah ... the thing is ... I'm still going to book a private session with him."

My eyes bugged out of my head like a cartoon character's.

"Are you serious, right now?! Lorna, come on! The guy is a complete scam artist! He's going to rip you off!" I picked up the card. "Two hundred and fifty dollars a session?! Unbelievable!"

"Yeah, but that's for the full hour — not the therapist fifty-minute hour."

The wave of rage had returned. "I don't want to insult you, Lorna, but you're an intelligent woman. How can you fall for this? It's a grift, plain and simple."

Lorna didn't look insulted. "I know it probably is. But it's entertaining, and I enjoy indulging in the idea of something bigger out there."

I bristled. "It's unconscionable."

Lorna remained unfazed. "No more so than the acting classes and headshots that coaches and photographers charge actors for when they come to L.A. I mean, they have to know when people are talentless, right? But they take their hard-earned money and feed them hope. How is that any different?"

Last week, I had paid a photographer in Winnetka over five hundred dollars for new photos that made me look like Willem Dafoe.

"It just is."

"You're right. We got free food and wine." She slowed the car down and put her right blinker on. "Ooh, speaking of, let's stop for *Hula Pie* at Duke's!"

While Lorna was conversing with the valet attendant, I had a closer look at that business card. In addition to the rates, there was an address: Mindanao Way, in one of the most expensive waterfront areas in Marina del Rey. And the "PH" before the apartment number boasted that the grifter in question was living in a penthouse.

I couldn't even afford the Hula Pie we were about to share.

* * *

A few days later, I was walking a white Bichon Frisé near the Mariners Village complex. Rover.com was just one of multiple websites I used to eke out an extremely modest living as an independent contractor. I was also on Taskrabbit, Instacart, and a weed delivery service called Leafly.com. Most of those deliveries were to Seth Rogen.

I was behind schedule and the Bichon was punishing me accordingly for being tardy, dragging me down Via Marina. Before I even clocked it, we were standing in front of the street sign for Mindanao Way. The Bichon was ready to turn back, but I dragged the little bugger behind me toward an address that was implanted indelibly upon my resentment-ridden brain.

The building was gorgeous: white stucco exterior with slate roof tiles and floor-to-ceiling windows. And the exquisite, pristine landscaping involved cherry-pink bougainvillea and immaculate putting-green turf. Most of the units faced the canal, and there were private boat slips leading right up to people's front doors. I shaded my eyes with my hand and tried to ascertain which of the penthouse windows belonged to Chief Redfeather.

"You need to get your act together."

I looked in the direction of the male voice. A florid senior in a golf shirt was pointing at the sidewalk, where Carmela the Bichon had taken a poop. I rummaged in my pockets for a bag.

"Sorry about that."

As I leaned down to pick up the deposit, I kept my eyes on that top floor, hoping to catch a glimpse of the con artist or anything else that would further fuel my fury. But the remote-controlled shades remained drawn, behind which HE was probably busy *not* working on his backstory. Then my phone rang. It was the Bichon's owner, wondering where I was because Carmela was late for her doggy acupuncture appointment.

I went back to that building every single day that week. I couldn't stop myself. No matter how hard Carmela pulled in the opposite direction. What was wrong with me? Wealth disparity was ubiquitous in L.A. County. It was simply something you had to make your peace with, otherwise jealousy would eat you alive. But I couldn't let it go. I started to despise the fraudster with an intensity that, up to then, I had reserved only for Michael Bay movies. It frightened me. He began to symbolize the injustice of every inequity in my life. At night I had dreams about killing him. One night, I pushed him off his wraparound balcony. The next night, we went out in his boat (I just assumed he had one), and I shoved him overboard, watching him sink into the inky water. The third night, I dreamed he lived, but his larynx was severed so that he could never do a terrible accent again.

At the end of every workday (every day for me), I would sit at my used IKEA dining table and make two columns on a piece of paper. In one, I would tally my income for the day. In the other, I would estimate how much he likely made, charging two hundred and fifty dollars an hour. The discrepancy was staggering — even factoring in the caramel brulée latte that he probably enjoyed every morning from the Starbucks in the lobby of his building.

I hated him.

I hated him.

I *hated* him.

The month passed slowly. Intense emotion serves to pull time out of shape, elongating it until it becomes endless. By the third week I had basically stopped showing up for my work appointments so that I could camp out on a bench below his building, hoping for a glimpse. But no matter how many hours I spent in situ, I never saw him. Not once.

So, I had no choice.

On the one-month anniversary of the salon, I took the funds I had set aside for my share of the utilities and used it to buy just enough gas to take me back to Topanga Canyon. Only this time I didn't have an invitation. I parked out on the pitch-black sideroad and hiked my way in.

I was early, so no guests had arrived yet. The driveway was empty. I sidled up the flagstone walkway, resisting the urge to punch one of the dreamcatchers. I stood on the front porch, trying to slow my breath ... trying to talk some sense into myself ... trying to leave.

But I couldn't.

I rang the doorbell — it was Pachelbel's Canon, of course — and tried to stop my hands from shaking. It was an eternity before I heard footsteps approaching. And then the heavy solid-oak door swung open and ***** stood there smiling, blissfully unaware of what was about to transpire in his home.

An hour later, he strode onto his makeshift stage and introduced me to the audience as Princess Enheduanna of Ancient Sumeria.

BIOGRAPHIES

EDITORS

SARA CHISOLM

Sara Chisolm is a speculative fiction writer based in the Los Angeles area. Her urban fantasy short stories "Serenade of the Gangsta," "The Fortune of the Three and the Kabuki Mask," and "We Found Love as the Undead," were featured in the second and third volumes of the *Made in L.A.* fiction anthology series.

GABI LORINO

Gabi Lorino is a writer, editor, and organizer of people, tasks, and information, currently based in Fort Wayne, Indiana. Her articles and short stories have been published in newspapers, websites, newsletters, magazines, and books. She has self-published one novel, *A Magical Time Called Later*, in addition to a journal series. She is a founding member of Made in L.A. Writers and serves as a co-editor for the *Made in L.A.* fiction anthology series.

ALLISON ROSE

Allison Rose is a novelist, screenwriter, and visual artist born and raised in Los Angeles. While Rose's stories vary in genre, the city often acts as a diverse backdrop for complex stories about female and LGBTQ+ characters and the deconstruction of tropes about women. Rose has worked in the entertainment industry in varying roles, including television production and music engineering. She is a founding member of Made in L.A. Writers and has used her twenty years of graphic design experience to create her own book covers, including every volume of *Made in L.A.* Recently, Rose has turned the lens onto herself in an upcoming memoir, which promises to be as darkly compelling and controversial as the figments of her imagination.

CODY SISCO

Cody Sisco is an author, editor, publisher, and literary community organizer. His LGBT psychological science fiction series includes two novels thus far, *Broken Mirror* and *Tortured Echoes*. He is a freelance editor specializing in genre-bending fiction and the acquisitions editor for RIZE Press. In 2017, he co-founded Made in L.A. Writers, an indie author co-op dedicated to the support and appreciation of independent authors. His startup, BookSwell, is a literary events and media production company dedicated to lifting up marginalized voices and connecting readers and writers in Southern California and beyond. He serves as a co-executive on the board of governors for the Editorial Freelancers Association and as a board member at APLA Health.

BIOGRAPHIES

CONTRIBUTORS

FRANK CASTELLUCCIO

Frank's dream has always been to write full time. He co-authored the biography of actress Vivian Vance, *The Other Side of Ethel Mertz* in 1998. He had every intention to keep writing, but when his life took a detour, his dream was put on hold. Many years later, he is finally back on the road he was meant to take and intends to stay on it. He now lives in Brooklyn with his husband, Ugo their dog, and Penelope, a cat who thinks she's a dog.

RYANE NICOLE GRANADOS

Ryane Nicole Granados is a Los Angeles native whose writing finds its roots in her love of community and her belief that Black motherhood is an act of social justice. She is inspired to write stories of survival that magnify the marginalized while also unearthing the splendor of second chances. Recently named the 2021 Established Writer and Individual Arts Fellow by the California Arts Council, her work has been featured in various publications, including *Pangyrus*, *The Manifest-Station*, *High Country News*, *The Atticus Review*, and *LA Parent Magazine*. Her storytelling has also been nominated for a Pushcart Prize and showcased in KPCC's live series *Unheard LA*.

SARAH HAUFRECT

Sarah Haufrect is a writer, communications director, and mental health advocate. She holds a BA from UC Berkeley and an MFA from Otis College of Art and Design, where she started the novel from which her story "The Makeup

Lesson" is an adapted excerpt. Since 2021, she has served on the board of directors for NAMI: WLA, the West Los Angeles affiliate of the National Alliance on Mental Illness. Recently, she was a 2021-22 BookEnds fellow through Southampton Arts — Stony Brook University. Sarah lives in Culver City with her husband, their dog, and over 10,000 comic books.

J.P. HIGGINS

J.P. Higgins, a denizen of the San Fernando Valley in Los Angeles, writes fiction and poetry to pique interest and curiosity, to elicit surprise and delight. Higgins's non-fiction interviews, business articles, and biographical sketches have appeared in both domestic and European magazines. His current project is a book-length biography of Isabelle Palms Buckley (1900-1986), the founder of The Buckley School where Higgins formerly served as Chairman of the Board of Trustees. He is a thirteen-year member of Independent Writers of Southern California (IWOSC). "Trouble Helping" is his second fiction piece to appear in the *Made in L.A.* anthology series.

CHRISTINA HOAG

Christina Hoag is the author of novels *Law of the Jungle*, *The Blood Room*, *Girl on the Brink*, and *Skin of Tattoos*, and co-authored *Peace in the Hood: Working with Gang Members to End the Violence*. A former journalist for the *Miami Herald* and Associated Press in Los Angeles, she reported from Latin America for major media including *Time*, *Business Week*, *New York Times*, *Financial Times*, and *Houston Chronicle*. Her short stories and essays have been published in numerous literary reviews, including

Toasted Cheese, *Lunch Ticket* and *Shooter*, and have won several awards.

TIARA ITO

When Tiara Ito is not writing, she's off somewhere thinking about it. Tiara lives, works, and writes from her home in Los Angeles, wrapped in her coziest blanket. With a background in Art and Design, she sees writing as a way to use words to paint on the page. She enjoys writing gripping tales about complex family relationships and the complicated emotions that remind us daily how human we are. She writes short stories and is experimenting with serial fiction while she completes her Creative Writing Certificate at UCLA Extension. Her story in this anthology is her first in the *Made in L.A.* series.

CATIE JARVIS

Catie Jarvis is an author of fiction, as well as a yoga instructor, a competitive gymnastics coach, an English and writing professor, a surfer, and a mom. She received her B.A. in writing from Ithaca College, and her MFA in creative writing from California College of the Arts. She grew up on a lake in northern New Jersey and now lives in Los Angeles with her husband, daughter Skywalker, and lots of surfboards. She finds the world to be a strange place and loves writing that examines the ambiguity of "reality." Her debut novel, *The Peacock Room*, is available on Amazon. This is Catie's second appearance in the *Made in L.A.* anthology series.

JOVON C. JOHNSON

Jovon C. Johnson was born and raised in Compton, California. Educated at San Diego State University, Oregon State University, and Antioch University Los Angeles, where he received an MFA in Creative Writing. He is a Kimbilio Fellow and the author of a poetry collection, *Keep Striving*. He assisted in the creation of the Kuumba Journal at San Diego State University. His work has appeared in *SoMa Literary Review*, *Caesura Journal* and *Elsewhere Lit*. He is an avid outdoorsman who spends most of his time getting lost in nature.

LAURA MCGHEE

Laura McGhee, a Canadian transplant, is an alumna of The Second City Theater and has a B.A. in French Literature — which has been super marketable. She has written several award-winning plays, which have been performed on CBC Radio, at the Just 4 Laughs Festival, and in venues in Halifax, Orlando, Minneapolis, Vancouver, New York, and L.A. Her television-writing career includes programs on CBC, CTV, and The Comedy Network. She has been nominated for a Gemini Award and a Canadian Comedy Award twice. She is also a certified airline transport pilot and a flight instructor. Her popular web series — "Lady Pilot" — explores the literal and figurative ups and downs of flying. And her first novel, *The Lineholder*, is based on her experiences as an airline pilot. Follow her somewhat ridiculous life at www.lady-pilot.com.

KARTER MYCROFT

Karter Mycroft is a writer, musician, game developer, and fisheries scientist who lives in Los Angeles. Their work has appeared in *Flame Tree Press*, *Ligeia Magazine*, *Apocalypse Confidential's* "Summer of the Shark" special issue, and elsewhere. Lately you can find them playing guitar into their computer.

NORIKO NAKADA

Noriko Nakada is a multi-racial Asian American who creates fiction, nonfiction, poetry, and art to capture the hidden stories she has been told not to talk about. Publications include her memoir series: *Through Eyes Like Mine*, *Overdue Apologies*, and *I Tried*. *Through Eyes Like Mine* was shortlisted for the 2040 Book Award. Excerpts, essays, fiction, and poetry have appeared in *Catapult*, *Meridian*, *Kartika*, *Hippocampus*, and *Linden Avenue*. She is a member of the leadership team for Women Who Submit, an organization empowering women and non-binary writers to submit their work for publication.

MARY ANNE PEREZ

Mary Anne Perez lives in Long Beach, California. She was chosen as a 2020 Writing By Writers Fellow and was long-listed in the Autumn 2021 Reflex Fiction competition. Her work has appeared in *Reflex Fiction*, *Shark Reef*, *Manifest-Station*, the *Los Angeles Times*, *Orange County Register*, and *Long Beach Press-Telegram*. She has read her work at the Billie Jean King Main Library and for the Womxn's Write Inn collective. She is writing a memoir about her family's service in World War II and a fairytale about a brown girl who climbs apricot trees and inherits a shawl knitted through the generations.

THEA PUESCHEL

Thea Pueschel is a writer that is equal parts technical and literary, a multi-media artist, yoga teacher, hypnotherapist, blog managing editor for Women Who Submit, a facilitator for Shut Up & Write, a California Arts Council Panelist 2022, and a Dorland Arts Colony Resident. Thea's published works can be found in *Short Edition*, *Perhappened*, and the WWS Gathering Anthology, among others.

TISHA MARIE REICHLE-AGUILERA

Chicana feminist and former rodeo queen, Tisha Marie Reichle-Aguilera (she/her) writes so the desert landscape of her childhood can be heard as loudly as the urban chaos of her adulthood. She is obsessed with food. A former high school teacher, she earned an MFA at Antioch University Los Angeles and is a PhD candidate at USC. Her fiction has been nominated for a Pushcart Prize, Best of the Net, Best Microfiction, and featured in *Best Small Fictions 2022*. Her YA novel, *Breaking Pattern*, is forthcoming with Inlandia Books. She's a Macondista and works for literary equity through Women Who Submit.

RYAN SHOEMAKER

Ryan Shoemaker's debut story collection, *Beyond the Lights*, is available through No Record Press. T.C. Boyle called it a collection that "moves effortlessly from brilliant comedic pieces to stories of deep emotional resonance." Ryan's fiction has appeared in *Gulf Stream*, *Santa Monica Review*, *Booth*, and *Juked*, among others. Find him at RyanShoemaker.net.

HAZEL KIGHT WITHAM

Hazel Kight Witham is a mother, teacher, slam poetry coach, and writer who was made in Los Angeles and still calls it home. She has published work in *The Sun*, *Bellevue Literary Review*, *Integrated Schools*, *Mutha Magazine*, *Cultural Weekly*, *Rising Phoenix Review*, and other journals. She is a proud public-school teacher in LAUSD and was a 2020 finalist for California Teacher of the Year. Since November 2008, she has shepherded more than two thousand students through National Novel Writing Month.

MADE IN L.A. WRITERS

Made in L.A. Writers is a collaborative of Los Angeles-based authors dedicated to nurturing and promoting indie fiction. While our styles, themes, and story locales differ, our work is both influenced and illuminated by our hometown and underpinned by the extraordinary, multifaceted, and often surreal culture and life in the City of Angels.

As indie authors, we face formidable challenges: fragmented audiences, intense competition in a crowded market, and traditional publishers' deep pockets.

If you enjoyed this book, please leave a review. Rave about us to your friends. Find us online and tell us how our stories made you feel. We're looking for connection; we hope to hear from you.

www.madeinlawriters.com

9 781953 954046